NO BRIDE PRICE

NOVEL BY DAVID RUBADIRI

no
bride
price

modern african LIBRARY

EAST AFRICAN PUBLISHING HOUSE
UNIAFRIC HOUSE, KOINANGE STREET
P. O. BOX 30571, NAIROBI, KENYA

First published in 1967

Printed in Letterpress by the
East African Institute Press Ltd.
Saldanha Lane, P.O. Box 30502
Nairobi, Kenya

For my children
Kwame, Sekou, Tengo
Desire, Lunga and Natasha
to whom Africa will
be a livable challenge

For my children

Krause, Sekou, Tenzo

Desta, Langston and Quanisha

to inherit Africa, and

be a livable challenge

Lombe moved about his little rented house with a glow of inward pride. It was in the African sector of the city. He was worried. He looked at himself in the mirror on the wall and lovingly fondled his new suit. He felt very proud of himself. Miria came into the bedroom and fussed around him.

Miria had walked into Lombe's life with the ease of most city girls. He had picked her up at the Astronaut. Slept with her for a day and decided to employ her as a housekeeper. She was tall and dark — very dark. Her features were sharply chiselled. Her eyes were round, possessing the innocence of a baby. When she first came she was wearing traditional clothing. This had suited her body and carriage. Now she wore European-type dresses which she carried with the awkwardness of an adolescent girl.

Like most city girls, Miria had left her village, and the only home she knew, to come to the city to look for a job as an ayah. She had walked through the whole length of the European and Indian sector looking for work.

Each time she had been asked for references. She had none. Eventually she found herself at the Astronaut. The bar-keeper had a sharp eye for these savage beauties. After a few words of praise and a well-laced bottle of beer, Miria had become a fixture at the Astronaut.

Lombe had received news of his promotion in the Labour Department on the day that he met Miria at the Astronaut. It had been a beautiful evening.

The excitement and beauty of that evening had continued as long as Miria played her part of being housegirl during the day and mistress at night. This had gone on well for about a month. But all of a sudden the arrangement had changed. Miria was tired of playing at girl house-keeping and, for all intents and purposes, was now mistress of the house.

"Why are you changing your clothes?" she asked.

"I told you never to ask me personal questions."

"Why not?"

"Because it's none of your business. These clothes are mine anyway."

Lombe brushed specks of cotton wool off his suit.

"Are you going out again?" Miria asked.

Of late, Miria had developed a strange possessiveness over Lombe. This irritated him. Each time he had come home after work he had told himself that it was time to chuck Miria out. She was getting too many fancy ideas.

"I told you that I'm a very busy man these days."

"But you do have working hours. Can't you stay with me for a few nights?"

"What do you want?"

"I am only asking," she replied lamely.

Lombe could no longer hold himself. "What do you want of me? I give you money; I buy you clothes: you are not my wife," he burst out.

8

She looked at him with a puzzled expression. Lombe turned aside to avoid her appeal.

"I simply wanted to talk to you."

"What have you got to tell me?"

She looked awkwardly around her, then said, "I went to the hospital this morning."

"And what has that got to do with me?"

An air of embarrassment crossed her face. She looked sideways and said, "I am carrying your babies."

The simple statement knocked Lombe hard. Was she trying to play city games with him? He would show her.

"What babies? What do you mean babies?" he shouted back.

She was afraid of him in this mood but decided that she must have it out with him.

"The doctor told me that I'm going to have twins."

"Twins?" he shouted back.

"Here are the hospital chits."

Lombe grabbed them. It was true. Miria was pregnant.

"You are lying," he shouted back.

To this she said in a quiet whisper, "The doctor told me that I can't have children the normal way."

"And so?"

"He said they will have to open me up."

Lombe looked at her with a pained face. Miria stood in front of him. Her face was stern and full of defiance as she saw him wriggling with the blow. Lombe pushed her roughly out of the bedroom. As she staggered and fell into the small room he used as his living room, he shouted at her, "How do you know that they are my babies anyway?"

Miria began to cry. Not the noisy African wailing. But crying with a shuddering of the body. Sobs that shook her like spasms. Tears fell on her chest and splashed down to where she was becoming big. Her hands and neck were taut with anguish. Lombe felt bitter gorge rise in him. He was ashamed to see her weep so. He felt angry and annoyed that he was caught.

He was a prisoner. Why, of all people, should it be him? He had been lonely. But so had she. He had wanted the warmth of a woman in his bed. He had done so much for her. Why had she done this to him? He had thought that she would appreciate his kindness. Kindness? Or was it the desire to find a woman at home whenever he came back from work? A woman who was so simple and self-giving. One that would save him the chore of chasing around every night. Now it had come to this. The invisible web of life had caught them unawares.

"Please, Lombe."

She shuddered.

"Don't think I've not appreciated all that has passed between us."

The anger in Lombe rose up to a fit of savagery.

"Try and understand, please. In my own way I love you," she said pleadingly.

Lombe could not withhold the fierce powers that were now possessing him. He shrunk at the word that had never been used between them — 'Love'. He suddenly recalled the times in the past when the word had been about to be used. He had countered such moments with calculated skill. After love-making, when everything was tender and the word lurked about them, Lombe had quickly turned rough. Pretended to lose his temper or introduced a topic that had turned tenderness into sordid business.

He looked at the dishevelled, weeping woman on the floor and spat out, "I wish to God I had never met you."

"I knew you were tired of me. I knew that. You now want to go to your other women."

The accusation stung Lombe. In himself he knew that he loved this mess of a girl now crawling under his feet. He knew it. But he was afraid. Afraid of what his friends would think; afraid of the future with this ignorant village girl. As she sobbed, her cloth dropped down, exposing a firm breast. Lombe felt a strange spasm of anger and lust arise in him. He tried very hard to control it. This was love and hate moving him. A blind wave of confusion overtook him. He struck her hard on the face.

Miria stood up, quivering with surprise and anger. Her sobs suddenly stopped. She looked at him with the pride that only the unsophisticated can master. She was fierce and beautiful to watch. With her firm breasts heaving up and down, she struck Lombe back. The blow rang out like the crack of a shot. Then like a demon she went about wrecking the little house. She threw chairs around, hurled books all over the place. Lombe tried to restrain her. She flung herself at him and tore his clothes to shreds, scratching him anywhere her sharp fingers could reach.

Lombe hit back hard. After a time she let go and collapsed on the floor. He slowly changed into another suit — straightened his tie and then left the house. He heard Miria's sobs through the window as he walked away from the house to the Astronaut.

The jukebox blazed away sixpences. In a corner of the
room were 'girls'. Heavy make-up gave them a neutral
expression. A mask that made them symbols of new
womanhood. The Astronaut made every woman significant.
It gave every girl a sex symbol. Behind their masks
they looked interesting, exciting, but, at the same time,
disgusting.

They wriggled in high-heeled shoes, their bottoms
bursting through their tight dresses. 'Bottoms' they called
them. The music gained momentum. The tight dresses
danced to the music. They bobbed up and down exposing
dirty underclothes and highly greased brown thighs. A
strong smell of sex engulfed the bar. The stench of
overnight urine drifted through the windows. Empty
bottles of beer lay about on ringed tables and on the floor.
Flies perched around unwashed glasses and old beer
bottles.

The music stopped. As the dancing girls flung themselves in exhaustion on the old couches they let off a strong smell of sweat and stale scent. Lombe felt the weight of the bodies as they thumped down. He was trying to make his beer last. These girls reminded him of Miria.

"Put on 'Julieta'," demanded the fat one in a loud, crude voice.

"Oh! I am sick and tired of 'Julieta'," shouted back the other.

"Put on anything then — the place is so dull."

The slim girl fumbled in her bag for a sixpence. Abandoning the attempt, she cast a provocative masked look at Lombe. Lombe tried to look impassive — but when she crossed her legs and made a half serious attempt to pull her dress down, he became uncomfortable. He reached for his half-filled bottle and poured out a jet of beer to fill the glass with froth, to give him time to let the froth settle down so that the beer could last.

"You are early today, Mr. Lombe," the fat girl said.

Lombe gave a grunt.

"Shall we put some music on for you?"

The two girls giggled. The fat one was drunk. She reached forward to remove his now almost finished bottle of beer, parting her legs in an obscene and seductive manner. Lombe could see the dark, torn knickers. He remembered the evening he had taken this particular girl out. She had been young like Miria — straight from the village. Her first dress had looked gauchy on her. Her body was used to loose cloth. Her skin was tight. She had a mysterious shyness about her. When he had taken her out again she had given him gonorrhoea.

"Shall I get you another beer, Mr. Lombe?" she asked provocatively.

"Not just now — I am waiting for a friend."

The two girls held hands and giggled. The fat one lunged forward and wriggled to the jukebox. She gave it a hard kick on its side and it started to blare again. The girls now danced separately — each looking far into the distance and slowly gyrating her waist and bottom, reminiscent of the village female dancer who dances to the compulsive appeal of the drummer.

Chaudry walked in suspiciously as the music came to an end. The two girls stopped dancing and looked at him with surprise and amusement. Indians never came to these places. He reached in his pocket for a cigarette. Lombe gave a loud cough. Chaudry saw Lombe and with relief walked to where he sat.

"What a swinging place, Lombe," he said rather nervously.

"Have you never been here before?"

"No — not really. I have only peeped in from my car on several evenings."

"What will you have?"

"A beer, please. Watching that dancing made me thirsty."

They laughed. Lombe gave the order for two beers with more confidence.

"You are a lucky man — to be able to come to night-clubs like this. My people would not be amused if they heard that I came to the Astronaut."

"What do you do in the evenings then?"

"Oh, mainly the cinema, or simply driving around and watching you chaps enjoy yourselves from the window of my car. There is, of course, the T. V.," he added.

The fat girl brought the beer. She stared deliberately at Chaudry as she opened it — then poured it out for him. The slim girl came over and stretched out her hand in shy greeting. Chaudry shuffled around in embarrassment as the girl put on the jukebox again and started dancing, as it looked, specially for him.

"I like the slim one, Lombe — she really is pretty."

"I never knew you were interested in girls, Chaudry — especially African girls."

"Don't be daft. What do you think I am — a saint or something, man!"

More people came into the room. Some waved to Lombe and nodded to Chaudry. The place began to get noisy as beer was downed to the hearty slapping of the girls' bottoms. Sammy, an acquaintance of Lombe, came over to join them.

"How's life, boy — you look rather serious today?"

"Not really, Sammy. How are you? Meet my friend Chaudry."

"How are you, sir?"

"How do you do, Mr. Sammy. Nice place, isn't it?"

"Yah! Thank the Almighty for it. Some of us would be carcasses without it."

"I dare say."

"Hey, Lombe — congratulations on your promotion and all that. Going up the ladder, eh! When do we celebrate?"

"Sammy boy — it looks like the break I've been waiting for. But what a hell of a time to wait for it — Independence so far away behind."

"What about us, old boy — still cringing to that white boss, not even a wink from the Perm. Sec."

"Come off it, Sammy! You have a decent chap as Perm. Sec. When is the sandwich filling going to get thinner?"

"Not a hope. Two more whites arrived today. Contracts for four years."

"Well, efficiency and integrity, old boy."

"Efficiency and integrity, my foot! One of these days I am going to find the chief a good little bottom so that he can at least give me a nod. Have a beer on me, big civil servant."

"Thanks, Sammy, we are about to leave."

"Mr. Chaudry?"

"No, thanks very much — we are going to a reception very soon."

"Reception!" Sammy repeated the words with rehearsed wonder. "Lombe, since when have you started to attend receptions? Must be the new privileges of office, eh?"

"Get off, man. Chaudry's father is the Indian High Commissioner and they are having a reception this evening — National Day of India."

"Good to meet you, Mr. Chaudry," Sammy snapped back. "I hope we shall see more of you. Lombe is a great friend of mine — are you sure you will not have just one on me?"

"No, old man — not today. Will see you later."

Chaudry and Lombe stood up to go. Sammy watched them leave — then turned to the fat girl who had been patiently waiting for him to finish.

"What is the matter with him?" she asked provocatively.

Sammy looked at her, gave her a large wink, squeezed her hard and ordered her to go and fetch another beer. The jukebox played louder as the Astronaut filled with more people and noise.

3

Lombe and Chaudry arrived at the lit gates of the
Embassy in the midst of a stream of traffic. A harassed
policeman was trying his best to direct the cars in an
orderly manner. But already one could see the shuffling
impatience of protocol making it difficult for him.

"They would all insist on coming according to degree,"
Chaudry muttered.

"What do you mean, according to degree?"

"Nothing really — customs of the diplomatic world."

Lombe felt excited. 'Customs of the diplomatic world.'
It sounded very grand and important. He had never been
to a function called a reception. Huge, black, shining cars
nosed their way towards the front door. Drivers jumped out
to open doors for rather bored, fat ladies and gentlemen.
He recognized the car of his Minister and of his Permanent
Secretary. He felt at once elated and scared.

Their car stopped and a uniformed attendant suddenly
appeared from nowhere to open their doors. Lombe hesitated

a bit — not knowing what to do or say. Chaudry flung himself out and shouted to the attendant, "Take the car to the back, Njoroge."

"Yes, sir."

"Come along, Lombe."

Lombe staggered after Chaudry into the main entrance of the brightly lit embassy.

"Don't bother shaking hands with my parents now. I'll introduce you later. Rather boring really — let's go and have a drink first."

Lombe followed blindly, tripping on the thick carpet at the entrance.

The room was filled with large bodies in dark suits and an assortment of glittering jewellery and expensive dresses. Everyone seemed to shout at no one at once. No one seemed to notice anyone. Chaudry weaved his way unconcernedly through the elegant crowd.

"Chaudry darling — aren't you going to say hello!" a voice said. It was more of an exclamation than a question.

Chaudry waved his hand and kept moving. Lombe followed determinedly, catching the last words as he passed.

"He's a sweet boy — isn't he?"

"What will you have, Lombe?"

"Oh! anything — anything."

"How about a large scotch and soda?"

"Yes, please."

"Waiter! two large scotches and soda, please."

"Hello, Chaudry," shouted a rather bilious large specimen propping up the bar. "Good to see ya."

"Hello, Al — enjoying yourself?"

"You bet," Al said, pushing around a large American bottom.

"Meet my friend, Mr. Lombe."

"Hello there now — my name is Al Sapone —

20

Information Attaché American Embassy — am sure mighty glad to meet you."

"Thank you, sir," muttered Lombe rather incoherently.

"I guess you are with the Minister here." A diplomatic thrust.

Before Lombe could begin to explain that he was in fact a Principal Secretary recently promoted in the Ministry of Labour, a cracking shout pierced the scene from behind him.

"Hello, old boy — splendid splash of saris, what?"

"Hi there — I was telling the gentleman here that this country is going to be really great."

Lombe felt a tug on his elbow. It was Chaudry forcibly propelling him to a quiet corner.

"Come and meet my sister. She teaches at the new school for children of diplomats."

Lombe felt rather relieved. He followed Chaudry across the room gingerly holding his drink as guests pushed about him and seemed to put their feet in his way each time he made a move. Half way through he caught the eye of his Minister. He mumbled a greeting and attempted a deep bow. The Minister calmly ignored him. In his embarrassment, his drink was knocked out of his hands and splashed down his jacket and trousers.

"Don't mind that. I'll get you another one. This way," said Chaudry. Lombe tried to apologize, at the same time fumbling for his handkerchief. A heavily made-up female looked at him with disgust. Lombe thought of the Astronaut and wished he was there at that moment.

* * *

Lombe was more relaxed sitting outside on the verandah with this interesting young lady. She had calmly led him out after Chaudry had introduced her as his sister. The noise inside was punctuated by wild peals of uninhibited

21

laughter. It had been frightening to Lombe at first. But after a few more stiff whiskies he felt more at home. The crowd drifted around itself. The same people meeting each other at every turn and speaking to each other as though they had just met.

"Quite a performance," thought Lombe. They seemed to do it so easily and yet, over all this, there was the overpowering atmosphere of boredom and pretence.

Lombe looked at Sandra. He was not at ease. He had never talked to an Indian girl before. Sandra was not what one might call a pretty girl. She was extremely handsome. Well-built. She was dressed in a red sari which she carried with the ease and elegance that only an Indian woman can manage. She spoke in a calm, low, lulling voice. It made Lombe think of his mother.

"Will you have another drink, Mr. Lombe?"

"Yes please, madam."

She brushed aside the 'madam' without any comment — but making it clear that she did not want him to call her madam.

"Do take one from the tray."

Lombe reached for another whisky. The waiter bowed slightly, inwardly amused at his trembling hand.

"I am so glad my brother introduced us. He talks a lot about you."

"He is a very good gentleman," he said.

"No one calls him that in this house." She giggled.

He liked the way she said that. Somehow it disassociated Chaudry from the frightening surroundings.

"I am very fond of him," she said, more to herself than to him.

"He tells me that you are very interested in African music and dances," she added.

22

"Yes, in a way. My late father was the chief musician at our chief's court."

"He told me that. He hopes that you will take him again to see the dancers."

"Certainly, any time. I like Mr. Chaudry very much. He understands."

The waiter quietly appeared again with the tray. Sandra helped herself to another sherry. Lombe felt an uneasiness creeping over him again. He looked nervously at his wet trousers.

"Quite a shower!" said Sandra, with a naughty gleam in her eyes. Lombe laughed out loud, more in relief than appreciation. He liked this girl. There was something reassuring and likeable about her.

"Do you like African music and dances?" he ventured to ask.

"I like music and dancing. I studied Oriental music and dancing at home. I am fascinated by your music and dancing though."

"Why?" asked Lombe.

"It has something old and fresh about it. Ours is so formed in many ways. Yours seems to be creative in time and place."

"What do you mean? I do not understand."

"Well, it is difficult to say what I mean. Perhaps..."

"Hello, Sandra, looking very beautiful tonight — gee, the way you kids look pretty in those saris amazes me."

It was the American diplomat. As usual he had to make his number with the mainstream of the source of power. Sandra took note of the remark with the ease and charm of disgust that only the well-bred can master.

"You too look very well, Al. I hope you're enjoying yourself." As an afterthought she added, "Have you two met?"

"To be sure. Mr. Lombe, isn't it? Mighty glad to make your acquaintance. Taking some fresh air, I guess. Boy, I can't get tired of these African evenings — aren't they beautiful?" He sighed.

"I am glad you like our country."

"Boy, do I like it." Al looked at the country in a trance.

Sandra stood up slowly and deliberately. "You must excuse me, I must go and help my mother."

"To be sure, Sandra, to be sure."

Al whistled a few lines from an uncomposed song, smiled emptily at Lombe and said, "I must go and pay my respects to Minister Chozo. Good to see you."

Lombe stood up, not knowing what to reply to the dismissal. The noise in the room was subsiding. There was a grinding of gears and revving of engines as the guests, in composed calmness but obviously in a hurry, tried to clamber in their cars to take their rightful protocol place in the departure queue.

"Have another drink, Lombe." It was Chaudry looking tired and bored. A half-drunk Italian girl was hanging on his arm, giggling delightfully.

"Hello, Mr. Minister." She waved vaguely at Lombe. "I vork for ze Minister of Vork?"

Lombe looked about him, not knowing what to say. The Minister of Labour suddenly appeared, rather unsteady on his feet. He gave a loud belch, and ignoring all the men around him, looked at the Italian girl from head to toe, undressing her by the stare, piece by piece, all the way down.

Chaudry pulled Lombe aside.

"You must be tired, it's a bit late. Come this way and I'll get one of our drivers to take you home."

Chaudry found a car for Lombe.

"I'll see you again tomorrow. You must come and see us. Don't wait to be asked."

"Thank you very much, Mr. Chaudry," said Lombe, "this has been a great day for me."

"Don't mention it — good night."

"Good night and thank you very much."

Lombe felt the glow of the whisky begin to spread in his belly. He had been uncomfortable at Chaudry's house. The presence of the Ministers and all the big people from the Embassies had made him feel uncomfortable. Secretly, however, he felt that it was a great thing that a simple person like himself should be invited to such a party. To actually go to a party with one's Minister and Perm. Sec. and then to be sent home in a chauffeur-driven car was a new and exciting experience.

He settled down in the cushy leather seats of the Benz and felt good. The driver slowly moved the car out of the Embassy gates.

"Which way, sir?" he asked politely.

Suddenly Lombe saw the absurdity of the situation. He did not want to tell this man that a big shot like him lived in the African sector of the town. He felt big and wanted to impress him.

"Which way, sir?" the driver asked again.

27

Lombe had to think of an answer quickly.

"Oh! I have a lot of work to do before I go to my residence. Drive me to my office near Barclays Bank."

The driver was suitably impressed and drove on fast to the centre of the city where all the big and impressive offices were situated.

"You drive the Ambassador, driver?" Lombe asked.

"No, sir, me just be assistant driver. I drive much the madam in town."

"I see," said Lombe in an important manner.

They left the dimly lit, fashionable suburbs of the town and drove into the main street of the city. Lombe wondered what he would do when they reached the Bank. It was a cool night and there were a few people walking on the pavement. There was very little traffic on the road. The big car ran quietly and smoothly. Lombe suddenly wished he was a Minister. No wonder these people did everything they could to get votes from the people. Then his mind switched over to his little house in the African sector of the town. He saw a heavy-eyed Miria waiting for him. The thought made him feel angry. Why had this primitive girl played tricks with him? He would show her. He would go back and tell her to return to the Astronaut. If she worked there for a week no one would believe the story that he had made her pregnant. If she tried to do so, no one would believe her. They knew the tricks that these girls played on young men who were getting on in government and in business.

The solution was so simple. Why had he worried so much about it? He planned every move carefully. He would go to the house and not speak to Miria. In the morning, he would tell her to go back to the Astronaut. If she refused to get out of the house he would call in the

28

police and tell them that she had stolen his money and was now refusing to leave the house. The threat should work.

The driver pulled in opposite the Bank. The street was deserted. To impress the driver Lombe jingled the keys in his pocket abstractedly. The driver left his seat in front and came to open the door for Lombe. He came out slowly, looking preoccupied. He turned sharply to the driver and said, "You can go now, driver."

"Thank you, sir." The driver saluted and drove off.

Lombe waited for the car to disappear into the night. The red lights at the back winked their way into the cool ambers of the street lights. Lombe was now alone. He felt cold and lonely. He had no money to take a taxi. The walk to his house would be about three miles. There was no alternative but to walk it.

The walk made him hot. He felt sober. He wondered why he had not asked the driver to drive him straight to his house. He found it painful to accept the truth. He only consoled himself with the thought that next time he went back to Chaudry's home the driver would spread the word amongst his friends that he was the big man at the Bank.

"You see that man there, Dickson?"

"No, man — who he be?"

"You not know him?"

"That one. Let me see. No, me not know him — who he be?"

"That be the big man at the Bank. He go there anytime to get money."

The driver would embellish the story to his friends.

He took off his jacket. He had now turned away from the main road on to a footpath that led to the African sector of the city. The grass was wet with dew. He stopped to roll his trousers up to his knees so that they would not get wet. The grass scratched his legs and made them itch. Frightened animals darted away from him into the bush as he walked along. Tomorrow he would put in his application for an advance to buy a car. The thought cheered him up.

There was a light in the house. That meant that Miria was there waiting for him. She had done this every day. He reached the corner of the house and paused for a moment to piss. At this time of the night the location was quiet. The good families slept early. The more active tenants were either at the beer houses, the Astronaut or visiting friends in other parts of the location. Next door someone was strumming a guitar and drunkenly singing about 'My baby doll.' He enjoyed pissing against the wall of his house. It gave him confidence and made him feel good. As he buttoned the fly of his trousers, a sharp, drunken voice of a woman pierced the night sharply. In the location one was used to women screaming. Voices of women being beaten by drunk husbands. Sometimes a man pleading with his wife to let him in and the wife declaiming loudly that she would not and that he had better go to his other woman. This voice tonight was claiming for money.

"You said you would give me five shillings."

"Shut up, woman," said the strong voice of a man.

"What do you think I am — a harlot?"

"Shut up you, woman, or I'll beat you up — beat you up so thoroughly that your mother will never recognize you again."

"You dare do that," she said at the top of her voice. "You dare do that if you are a man. Give me my money," she demanded.

"Shut up, woman," he kept on saying.

"No. I will not take your one shilling — what do you think I am, a harlot?" She repeated the word 'harlot' with indignant loudness.

"Shut up, woman, before I smash you."

"Truth God, I am not going out until you give me my money."

"Then come back to bed if you are not going away," he said with bilious pleasure.

There was a noisy scuffle as the two naked bodies came to grips — rudely pushing furniture and beds in the dark. The heavy breathing could be heard even where Lombe stood. There was a loud thud as they fell down on the bed. Then silence.

Lombe finished buttoning his fly and prepared to enter the house. The door was open. He had expected to find the mess that he had left in the evening after the quarrel with Miria. The sitting room looked tidy. Miria had replaced the books on the shelves. As usual, some titles were upside down. She had even smoothed Lombe's ruffled suit. The great moment had come. He prepared to enter the bedroom and face Miria. With an air of self-confidence he pushed the door leading to the bedroom and stood square in it looking for Miria sitting on the bed waiting for him.

Miria had gone.

Lombe was full of elation as he walked into his new office the next morning. The pile of files in the 'IN' tray made him feel important. They were old files inherited from the former colonial government. They all requested the old forms of action, officer, date, initials, action taken, pending, urgent, immediate action. It all looked very impressive to Lombe. He looked at them and sighed with pleasure. Two telephones stood on a side table. One was a direct line to the Perm. Sec. He looked at it and waited for the ring that would summon him to the chief. A messenger came in at regular intervals to busy himself with habitual little chores.

The desk was typical of the old colonial administrative officers. Readable scrawls of golf engagements. Telephone numbers and little drawings.

"Tea, sir?" asked the messenger.

"Yes — with milk," he said, "and messenger!"

"Yes, sir?"

33

"Tell my secretary not to disturb me except for very special calls — do you understand?"

Lombe felt good. You had to impress these messengers otherwise they would become cheeky. His mind was on the telephones. He wanted to try his new authority voice in them. He fondled the files — afraid to open them. Somehow he felt that they contained new mysteries of himself and his new position. The chair was firm and good. He adjusted the knot of his tie. How would he receive visitors? He cleared his throat and tried it to himself.

"Come in — do sit down, please." That sounded like a good start.

"What can I do for you, Mr. Chikoko? Of course, yes. I know your case. I shall have to refer the matter to the Minister first." Good enough, but it sounded rather servile. He tried a more aggressive approach.

"What is your name? What do you want — did you make an appointment?" That sounded more impressive. Why did the telephones not ring?

Suddenly he felt lonely in this room. The thought of taking action on his own without someone telling him what to do frightened him. Suppose he did the wrong thing? The Perm. Sec. had told him that whenever he was in doubt on any matter he should consult him. He knew, however, that reluctance to take action was a sign of lack of initiative. Slowly he picked up a file and opened it. The subject of the file was Mr. Zoze Chikoze, Secretary General, Motor Workers Union.

Lombe knew old Chikoze. A fiery Trade Unionist. Full of ambitions to use the workers to get into politics. Otherwise he was harmless and more happy playing at drinks and girls. The file described Chikoze as a definite danger to the security of the nation. A man to be closely watched. This time the Minister had called for a special report on Chikoze. Lombe had to write it. Lombe visualised old Chikoze dead drunk at the Astronaut. He saw Chikoze performing at a workers' rally. A brilliant speaker and rabble rouser. That was what had kept him on top in the Union. If only they could vote him into parliament that would finish old Chikoze. The telephone rang. The messenger came in to watch. Lombe was too excited to talk to him. He hurriedly reached for the receiver, then remembered that it was more dignified and impressive to let the phone ring for some time. He slowly drew his hand away and pretended to be reading the files. Then he turned to the telephones with an impatient look. He could not guess which of the two was ringing. He made a bold gesture and picked the wrong one. In his excitement, he talked hard into the telephone while the other kept on ringing.

"Hello — Mr. Lombe here — Ministry of Labour... Hello, Mr. Lombe here — Ministry of Labour... Hello, Lombe — Secretary Labour Ministry... Hello... Hello ... Hello."

A sly smile crossed the face of the messenger. He pointed to the other telephone. Lombe, now in a panic, reached for it desperately.

"Mr. Lombe?" It was the girl at the exchange.

"Hello, Ministry of Labour, Mr. Lombe."

"Hello — is that Mr. Lombe?" the girl asked again.

"Yes, sir. Lombe speaking," he mumbled into the phone.

"Hold on, sir, I have a call for you."

Lombe waited, trying to settle himself. He wondered who this caller would be.

"Hello, Lombe," a voice said.

"S-p-e-a-k-i-n-g."

"Is that you, Lombe?"

"Lombe speaking here," he barked into the phone.

"Oh, this is Chaudry here."

"Oh yes, Mr. Chaudry." He suddenly felt small.

"Just a small matter about Saturday."

"Yes, Mr. Chaudry." He wanted to say 'sir'. 'Mister' and 'sir' had become a habit to him when addressing anyone white or yellow.

"Do you mind if Sandra came along as well? She would very much like to come with us."

"Yes, Mr. Chaudry, Sandra must come too."

"Splendid," said Chaudry, obviously pleased with the news, "we shall pick you up outside the Astronaut."

"Yes, outside the Astronaut," he mumbled with excitement.

"Thanks awfully. Sorry to bother you, you must be busy."

"Not at all." He managed to withhold the 'sir'.

Lombe hung on to the telephone after Chaudry had stopped talking. Now he felt he could handle the instrument. He particularly liked that bit about being busy. He began to plan the Saturday trip to his village with Chaudry and Sandra. It would look very impressive arriving in a Benz at the village. He could see the children crowding round the car; the surprised grown-ups. They would all then know that Lombe's son had risen in the world. The thought of travelling with Sandra elated him. Why did the truth bore into him so much? Yesterday he had talked to her and she had reminded him of another girl. One who looked like Miria but had the carriage and sophistication of Sandra. Secretly he felt a longing for Sandra. But she was an Indian and no one could ever really get to know an Indian girl.

If only she were not an Indian he would have proposed to her. She was so much like the Miria he wanted. The thought of Miria brought back pain and anger. Where had she gone to? Suppose she had gone back to the village and told her people the story. The idea made him more angry. If she had gone back to the village then the Saturday visit would be tragic. Why should all this happen to him — and at this particular time? Why was this girl demanding his soul? Why did she allow herself to become pregnant? Most bar girls got pregnant but they never made a fuss about it.

The internal telephone rang.

"Mr. Lombe?"

"Speaking."

"The Permanent Secretary here."

"Yes, sir."

"Could you come to my office for a few minutes, please."

This was the summons that he had been waiting for. He straightened his tie. With a spring in his step he strode out to see the Perm. Sec.

Lombe tried to return straight to his house that evening. Secretly he knew that he wanted to see Miria again. He wanted very much to say how sorry he was. To tell her that if she would agree to go back to the village he would send her money every month. Nothing seemed to ease his mind and blot out Miria. A sense of shame crowded all his thoughts. A sense of guilt made him feel helpless. It was not pride that made him feel this savage resentment against Miria. He knew that he loved her. It was this fear of the town and of the times. What would his friends think?

Each time he came near his house he turned away from it and walked some distance away. In a moment of desperation he decided to go to the Astronaut. It was late in the evening. The boys were all there.

"Here comes the great chief." It was Sammy. As usual already worse for drink. His shirt needed a new collar. He smelt strongly of alcohol and of sweat and the dust that cakes one from bicycling long distances. He needed a bath.

"Have a beer, old man. Good to see you once in a while," Sammy said. He shouted at the fat girl to bring the beer. They drank in silence for some time.

"What is the matter with you these days, Lombe? You are very quiet — anything the matter?"

"Nothing really, Sammy. I am just feeling sort of tired."

"Come off it. You can't fool me, I know you well enough." He poured out the rest of the beer and ordered some more.

"No, Sammy. It's my turn. I'll pay for this lot."

"As you wish." The fat girl brought the beer. She leered at Lombe with a come-hither-kid look. Are you a man or not? Before Miria, this kind of challenge would have sent Lombe on a bull's charge.

"Six shillings, Mr. Lombe," she cooed.

"Tell me, old man, anything wrong at work or is Miria giving you hell?"

It was no use. He might as well tell him everything.

"I am in trouble, Sammy."

"Then why all this?"

"It's Miria," Lombe said looking at his friend.

"I thought so — drink up. Have you planted the seed in her?"

"Well, it's something like that."

"What do you mean, something like that? Either you have or somebody else has, old man."

The suggestion that somebody else could have done it stung Lombe. It was like passing judgement for murder. He wished in one moment that it had been someone else and not him. But a pang of fear made him realize that he could never stand anyone fooling around with Miria. He wished for an explanation of the forces that had made his life so full and yet so shabby and empty.

40

"I am surprised at the way you take it. Did you expect a bar girl to stay chaste all the time for you?"

Lombe drank up his beer and ordered another round.

"Boy — just make a visit to the water works — they drag them out before even the tails are off. That's where they leave them, to the City Council."

Lombe shuddered at the thought. He looked at the bar girls dotted round the room. They looked like a huge mockery on all the men that were drinking and pinching their bottoms. They had completely, as it were, dispossessed themselves of their bodies. Their bodies were used like the old cushions around them, to be pinched and sat upon. Their souls felt like the stuffing that took the weight and the beating from the bottoms that farted on them.

"Why don't you do the obvious, man?"

"What do you mean?"

"Get rid of the thing, of course."

"But..."

"Shut up, man. I know a fellow who can do it for you for 150 shillings. Shall I arrange it?"

"But I am not sure whether..."

"Don't worry about it. He is a doctor. As a matter of fact I have an engagement with an interesting group tonight. I would like you to meet them. Free booze. I provide the dames. He will be there. Let's have a couple more drinks and we'll be off."

The idea appealed to Lombe. The beer had washed away the agonies of worry. Why not try it? It would be the perfect solution. In a few days Miria would be rid of the bother. He would have collected his new car and then would tell her to leave his place. If she refused he would call in the police.

"You are too young to be tied up with these town tarts, man, they suck you dry and then leave you." Lombe listened patiently. He was feeling fine now. Sammy was expressing his thoughts and easing his sense of guilt for him.

"You have a great future, man. Me," Sammy said, "I know my lot. I don't try to fight it. I shall not get anywhere far, so I do the best with it. When the politicians want me to go and shout and clown at their meetings I do so. When my boss wants dames, I provide them. No one asks me then about my inefficiency or why my clothes are not presentable. But you are smart, Lombe. One of these days I'll be calling you 'sir'."

Lombe managed a smile. He felt good. He was glad that people like Sammy could recognize his great potential.

"Here comes Brute — let's be off."

With a showy grinding of tyres they rode off in Brute's old, battered Anglia.

Brute pulled out a bottle of brandy, bit off the top, took a good draught from it and passed it to the back. "Groceries, gentlemen." Sammy grabbed the bottle, heaved a long drink from it and passed it on to Lombe.

"That's fire. I can feel it going down all the way, Brute. Great stuff. Don't tell me it's South African. I don't want to vomit."

"No, Sammy, I have changed the label."

"Good show. We don't want any of these young brigades to get fancy on us, do we?"

They laughed heartily as Brute manoeuvred his car over unimaginable little pathways.

"Which lot first, Sammy?" asked Brute, chewing lovingly at his cigar.

"Let's collect the pros first. Be sure we have done our job."

"You are right. Thing is if you do not collect them first there's always a cold war with the fancy ones."

Sammy dug a hefty nudge in Lombe's side.

"Where are the groceries? Be a good chap and pass them forward."

The bottle of brandy was passed. Lombe noticed that the label was sticky and coming off. He quietly pasted it on the back and passed the bottle to Brute.

"Which fancy set this time, Sammy?"

"The hospital set, man. They are good sport. George tells me he is expecting some high folk tonight. Business and Diplomacy."

They all laughed heartily. "Business and Diplomacy then it shall be," said Sammy.

The old car crashed through potholes and grass verges to its destination as the 'groceries' were again passed around.

Lombe had never been to this kind of party before. The room was large and artistically arranged. All around the room people sat in twos and fours, drinking and talking loudly. The lights were so dim that it was difficult to see the faces of the people well.

"Hi, Sammy — you there too, Brute, good to see you folks." The rather bilious voice came from a large and ebullient American.

"Hi, George, good to see you. I have brought a few friends, I hope you don't mind."

"Not at all, come all in — we sure wouldn't mind more company."

George gave Sammy a conspiratorial wink. Sammy introduced Lombe and the girls. It was quite clear that the girls were used to this kind of party. A number of the men took them away as soon as they saw them. The girls giggled most of the time.

"Go help yourself to some drinks, Sammy," said George.

"Sure thing," said Sammy. "Come along, Lombe."

The table was loaded with drink. He had never seen so many bottles of different kinds of drinks. Sammy surveyed the scene and looked pleased.

"They really mean business tonight."

"Who are these people, Sammy," asked Lombe.

Sammy looked around the room. "The high and the mighty," he said slowly. "George, our host, is what they call a First Secretary at the American Embassy. Saleh there, with the fat girl, is the Sudanese Consul. The small fellow writes the British Information News for you. The white girl is a secretary. The Indian owns the money of this country. The rest you will get to know soon. What will you drink?"

"Whisky and soda, please."

"That's the stuff. You have to prepare yourself for this kind of party."

They took their drinks to a less populated part of the room. George stood up, rather unsteady on his feet, and went to put a twist record on the gramophone.

"This place needs warming up a bit. How about a twist, folks?"

A general assent was mumbled. Chubby Checker was put on.

"We are off!" said Sammy.

"What do you mean?" asked Lombe.

"Just watch — the party has started. Close your eyes if you are under age."

George was moving fast towards the slim, tall nurse, Agnes. She was dressed in a tight, short dress which showed her body to best advantage. She smiled provocatively at George and stood up to dance. She danced gracefully. The music oozed through her limbs.

46

"Baby — this is just crazy — just crazy — isn't she great?"

She did not look at him as they danced. Her twist was boneless, flowing like a snake. In contrast with George's cerebral desire and calculated abandon, the two figures sharply defined two worlds. Funny that in the dim lights of a neutral room Africa played strange scenes of a drama that plain daylight made so painfully difficult.

Lombe looked at Sammy. He was not taking much notice of what was happening. Lombe looked around the room again and was fascinated with the way the Sudanese Consul was carrying on with one of the fat girls they had brought to the party. The Consul was completely taken by the girl. Obviously he was whispering some sweet obscenities in her ear. She loved every minute of it. She wore a very tight dress which kept moving up her knees exposing ebony thighs and a red petticoat. Sammy saw his friend observing the scene with interest.

"They call her 'Danger'," he said.

"Who?"

"The girl you are looking at. She is a pro and specializes in whites and Indians only."

"You mean she won't go out with Africans?"

"Nop. It's not chic. Besides you Africans demand too much charity and make them pregnant in no time. You have no science."

The music stopped. George hung on Agnes' arm, pulling her over to the gramophone to put on another record. Sammy poured himself and Lombe another drink. George and a few more couples started on a creeping dance. Here George excelled but Agnes was obviously uncomfortable at being trapped in a dance that made the body prisoner to the music.

"Sammy, do you come to these places often?" asked Lombe.

"Nearly once a week. They are fun. Free drink — you get a lot of information and sometimes a white woman picks you up."

"And you go?"

"Sometimes," he said musingly.

"And others?"

"I don't. They can be very possessive once they get you and their men genuinely don't like it. That can spoil friendships."

Sammy left Lombe to go and speak to an elegant looking Indian who had just walked in. From the distance he saw the figure of an attractive, middle-aged, white woman slowly walking towards him. She looked neat in a tight fitting black dress. She came straight to where Lombe was sitting.

"Hello," she said.

"Hello," Lombe said, trying to get up. A matter of habit he had acquired from his years of education. She put a hand on his shoulder and elegantly eased herself on to a cushion next to him.

"I have seen you before," she said. A whiff of strong scent crossed Lombe's nose. A brush of blonde hair tingled sharply against his cheek

"I don't know, madam," he said.

Sharp blue eyes looked straight into Lombe's, saying, "How very green."

"You are very nervous," she said. "My name is Moira. What's yours?"

"Lombe — Jonathan Lombe."

"Lovely names. Are you enjoying the party?" she asked with a touch of mockery.

"It is wonderful to meet all these important people here," he said lamely.

She laughed quietly at this. Lombe tried to understand her reaction to his statement. He had sat next to white women before but they had always felt uncomfortable and talked too much to ease the tension. Moira looked calm and composed. He could feel her presence. It was a warm presence but one which was not entirely at ease in this particular room. She must come to this kind of thing out of boredom or simply to be around people.

"Do you know any of these people?" she asked.

"No — not all of them," he lied. The only people he knew in the room were Sammy and the girls they had come with. The diplomats and the others he was meeting for the first time.

"Just as well," she said. "They are all sick."

"Sick?"

"Yes. Sick — here." She pointed to her head and watched Lombe trying to work out the riddle. Lombe tried to understand. She kept on looking at him.

"Hello, Moira —." It was the sharp voice of the English diplomat. "Care for a dance?"

"No thanks, Bruce, not now." She turned sharply away from Bruce, making it quite clear that she did not want him to hang around.

"He's a pain in the neck," she said.

"Why?"

"He's always trying to be protective".

"Is he your husband?"

"No — you're kidding. He just thinks that I might jump into bed with Africans. He's a queer."

"A what?"

"A queer. He sleeps with little black boys."

This was the reaction Moira had been waiting for from Lombe. Lombe was genuinely shocked at the ease with which this woman discussed such things. He had heard stories of this kind from Sammy but never took them seriously. Most of them were in connection with Roman Catholic priests.

"You look surprised," she said.

"Yes, I am — I never knew that it was possible."

"You are a real man," she said.

Lombe kept quiet. He was feeling uncomfortable. No woman had ever talked to him like this. Moira had taken too many liberties talking to him like this. Normally he should have felt angry and insulted. What did she think he was? In the old days her menfolk would have given him orders or talked to him like a little boy. Now that the terms of personal relationship had changed, the menfolk seemed to take licence and use them for interests that, at most, were very much on the surface and frivolous. The woman tried long-whispered myths. He could be rude and crude to her. She would love that. What a world of difference between Miria and Moira. And yet she was different. She now sat quiet, looking at him smoking a cigarette. This woman certainly knew her sex. She had, at one time, been proud of being a woman, much as Miria and Sandra were proud all the time of being women. Some silly man must have abused her. He must have refused to accept the responsibility of his manhood and had, as a result, abused the woman in her.

"You think I need a man," she said.

Lombe felt annoyed that he was one step behind each time this woman talked to him.

"Miss Moira, everybody needs somebody."

"It is true. Much more so in Africa. Africa can be a painful paradox, you know. Even those who come to Africa to be themselves eventually come down to the basic truth — the loneliness that is in the community." She looked thoughtful. "We came and killed your community with our ideas of the individual and now we are busy

50

discovering, after the tragedy, from those who can no longer give it back, the greatest thing that kept Africa."

The dancers had long abandoned the shake. They were creeping round the floor in slow motion. The gap of understanding had disappeared when the strength of body touching body had thawed, obeying laws of magnetism.

"Have you got a girl friend?" she asked. It was an innocent question. Lombe had never understood what foreigners meant by the phrase 'girl friend'. To him a friend was a man. A woman was something infinitely different.

"I am sorry. I was not trying to pry into your private life — forgive."

The blue eyes played sharply on Lombe's face. The sharpness turned to tenderness. An understanding of minds passed through them. Lombe felt a spasm of pity and respect for this woman. She smiled faintly at him, then slowly reached out a hand towards him. It was warm and moist.

"Let's dance," she said.

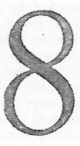

It must have been something to do with the softness
of the bed. It must have, perhaps, been the odd smell.
But Lombe woke up from sleep at the crack of dawn and
found himself sleeping in a strangely cool and soft
bed. At first he thought he was dreaming and wished to
linger on in the dream. But like all lovely dreams the
jolt to consciousness was sudden. He sat up and
looked round about him. The long, warm curtains on the
window assured him that he was not sleeping in his house.
Beside him lay the figure of a white woman. Peaceful,
with the countenance of a child. Below the sunburnt
neck was the smooth, white body of a woman. Terror
struck first. Then the slow process of thought brought the
story of the previous night back.

Moira slept with the peaceful face of a baby. Her
blonde hair spread on the pillow in bright streaks of
abandon. Her mouth was slightly parted and she breathed
in short gasps. Lombe did not want to disturb her. He

was frightened to wake and face her. He remembered the whispered demand 'let's dance', then the close, clumsy cheek to cheek dance. The weight of Moira's bosom as they danced had put fire into him. The savage demands in bed had first been repulsive to him. Demands of a starved, beautiful beast. But he had given in to them.

Suddenly panic overtook him. He got out of bed and started to dress. Slowly and nimbly he pulled on his trousers. In the midst of trying to be quiet he knocked the side of the bed and Moira woke up.

"Is that you, Lombe?" Moira said half asleep.

Lombe stood still. He did not know how to talk to her again. He wanted to get out of this room and the house as quickly as possible and go to the location. Back to the home and to the values that he could understand.

"Is that you, Jonathan?" she asked again — wriggling from the bed and trying to clear her eyes to see Lombe.

"Yes," he said. "I must go now," he said in a pleading voice.

An awkward silence came between them. Lombe hurriedly finished dressing. He was not looking at her.

"Come here," she said. Lombe meekly walked to the side of the bed. She reached an arm towards him. Lombe felt helpless but, at the same time, repulsed by the gesture.

"Watch them, they possess you when they get you." The words came ringing in his mind. He felt rotten. She had given much of herself and he had allowed himself to be used. He saw Miria sprawling on the floor of his house in the location weeping after the fight, the tears falling down to where she was big.

"You are still nervous," she said, pulling his head towards her face to kiss him. He pulled away.

"I must go now or I will be late," he said.

She clung tight to him, then let him go.

54

He was breathless as he knocked on Sammy's door. Sammy was still in bed. After a number of desperate knocks a sleepy Sammy came to open the door. He had on a dirty bed-cover. He did not like the idea of being pulled out of bed at such an early hour. He cast one quick look at his friend and said, "Come in."

Lombe walked meekly into the room.

"So you have been caught," he said.

Lombe did not say a word. He just sat down on a chair and looked at the ground. Sammy went to his petrol box and helped himself to a drink.

"I feel scared, Sammy," Lombe said.

"Scared of what? Of sleeping with a white woman?"

"Don't be so cruel, Sammy. It's not that."

"What then?"

"I don't know, Sammy. All these things happening to me. I am scared."

"Some people would feel proud. They call it paying the national debt." Sammy said the words with an acid spit.

"Can I use your basin to wash? I have got to go to work."

"The old Pilate. You can go and wash your hands, Lombe."

Lombe did not like his friend's comment. The confusion was not that he was scared. The confusion was that he had done something which gave him a feeling of guilt. A gnawing guilt and feeling of shame, not only that he had lacked the courage to resist an animal instinct but had betrayed himself, and Moira, and Miria.

"You are trapped, man — well and truly trapped," Sammy said. Lombe did not reply.

"Now that you have paid the national debt how about the home girl, eh?" Sammy kept taunting.

Lombe picked up Sammy's basin. He filled it with cold water and went out in the yard to wash himself. He tried to make sense of his friend Sammy. But he, too, was elusive like everything that was happening to him.

At times Lombe had worried about what Sandra and
Chaudry would think about his village when they actually
got there. He was proud of it, of course. But his mind was
too coloured with the word values that had always been
used in describing his people — especially those who lived
in the country. The fact that his people would not be
able to speak in English worried him. The fact that
there would be a lot of dirt and plain nakedness nagged him.
But home was home. He wanted these two people, whom he
had taken to heart, to meet his mother. He was very proud
of her and through her he wanted to establish a meeting
point of mutual understanding and respect. In the city he
could not do this because his life had been so arranged for
him by powers now gone that he would for a long time
remain a recipient, an observer and a thank-you man.
Secretly too, he wanted to show the village that Lombe's son
had got on in life. The sense of inadequacy gave way to one
of expectant joy, of fulfilment.

As Saturday approached, the events of the past week began to loose the sharpness of initial shock. He began to get used to the fumes of cocktail parties and the small talk that went with them. He had stopped trying to work out the meaning of the night he had spent at Moira's. He had even stopped worrying about the day when he had met Moira in the streets in town. She was with some of her friends. Their eyes had met but she had completely ignored him.

Sandra, on the other hand, was constantly in his mind. She was a mystery dressed always in a red sari. A woman present yet aloof. She presented a kind of purity that frightened him the more because she also reminded him of Miria. The two women had now driven him to heavy drinking. His work at the office became indifferent and he was in debt.

The journey to Lombe's village was punctuated with the usual sentiments of scenery appreciation. The three people tried to ease off their fears and concerns with polite conversation. Lombe was particularly talkative, pointing out one thing of interest after another. Chaudry and Sandra appreciated eveything that was pointed out to them with enthusiasm.

The usual swarms of children greeted the arrival of the big car from the city. Lombe was pleased by the welcome. Chaudry and Sandra were overwhelmed by the invasion. Dirty faces and dirty hands grabbed at the car and peered with broad smiles through the windows.

"We cannot go further than this. We shall have to leave the car here," Lombe said.

They got out. Crowds of children, curious, chatty and scared, followed them to the village. They passed by goats feeding near the huts. Chickens made a path for them as they approached. Women paused in their chores as they passed them with Lombe tossing respectful greetings to them.

"We are very near my mother's house now," he announced.

"Oh, I am so excited," said Sandra in a rather shrill voice. A foreign voice piercing through the African sounds of the children. The procession of children and thin dogs followed.

"They are very happy to see you," Lombe said, giving them a broad smile.

"They certainly look happy," Sandra said. Chaudry did not say a word all the way to Lombe's mother's hut.

Lombe's mother was at a neighbour's house when they arrived. Lombe sent a small boy to go and call her. As the boy went to look for her a chorus of women calling 'Malombe' started all around them.

"MaLombe eeh."

"MaLombe uuu."

Lombe looked at his friends and smiled.

"They are calling my mother."

"I thought so. They look very pleased to see you."

"This is wonderful, Lombe," coughed out Chaudry as the dust hit his throat.

Lombe's mother came, looking very excited and pleased. She paused to look at her son and then opened the door of the hut and let the visitors in. Lombe motioned to Sandra and Chaudry to enter.

It was cool in the hut. It was simply laid out and neat. Sandra and Chaudry were dutifully sat on two stools. Lombe sat near them on a mat. Lombe's mother sat some distance away from them on a goat's skin.

She was an extremely handsome old woman. Years of producing children and doing the heavy family chores had flattened her chest but the handsome lines of her youth were still decipherable. She sat very calm on her skin, not looking at anyone in particular.

"My mother wishes to greet you," Lombe said.

Chaudry made as if to stand up. She pinned him down on his stool by rising up from the floor to her knees. She stretched a hand to Chaudry and then to Sandra, not saying a word. Then she spoke to them through Lombe.

"I hope you had a good journey," she said.

"Yes, mother, a very good journey."

"I am pleased."

"And you, mother, I hope you are well."

"As you see, my son. As well as an old woman can be."

There was a pause. Each communing with their own thoughts and meeting silently through the pause.

"You have brought us some visitors," she said.

"Yes, mother. They are my friends in town. Children of a very important person from India — very far away across the seas."

"We are pleased you have brought them. I am sorry that we cannot put them in a better place."

Lombe interpreted this to Sandra and Chaudry. They listened with respect.

"Tell her," said Sandra, "that we feel very honoured to be received by her and to be in her house."

The sentiment pleased Lombe's mother very much. For the first time she smiled back at them and looked at Sandra.

"Tell her," she said, "they are very welcome to this house."

Just as she had come she stood up and, half bending, she left. This was the sign for the villagers to come in and greet the visitors and Lombe. They came in what seemed a never-ending stream. They came in and sat down, shook hands, looked down, then quickly took a fleeting glance at the visitors and left. Outside could be heard giggles. It was a good sign — they liked them. Lombe looked pleased that they had been well received.

Lombe had brought Sandra and Chaudry to the village on the day that the village came together to celebrate. An evening where the village sang songs, danced and the men drank beer. It was difficult to explain to anyone why such evenings happened. They came like a sudden showed of rain after a long spell of dry weather washing away the dirt and the bits and pieces of garbage. Like a full shower, it washed the well-worn foothpaths and smoothed the roughened grass on the huts and made the earth smell sweet.

The village had quietly prepared for the evening long before Lombe and his party arrived. Their arrival was taken as a good omen and added more to the excitement that was to come. The day-to-day and the mundane were going to be temporarily put aside and the village was going to communicate. Day after day, the daily business of living had gone on. There had been deaths and births, burials and marriages. Quarrels had been discussed at length and settled. The young had been initiated. Months of waiting for the young boys who had gone to the big towns had passed. Many had come back with some money, bicycles, tin trunks, sun-glasses and secondhand suits bought from Indian stores that specialized in selling clothes from Europeans who went back to their country on leave or for good.

The young men caused quite a stir when they came back. They got married, tried their hands in business, lost all the money they had made in the towns and patched up their old, secondhand, baggy dinner suits. The city stories ceased to fascinate and they wandered around the village drinking and feeling rather sorry for themselves. An evening like the one to come would rejuvenate them into life again, wear away the gloom that they had cast over those who had stayed, now called upon to cheer them. This was the secret understanding of the village. This was the way the soul of the village looked after its people.

"They are having a dance tonight," said Lombe.

"How wonderful," said Sandra. "Not specially for us I am sure."

"Not really, Miss Sandra — but it will also be for you because it's for everybody."

Chaudry looked excited. Sandra felt relieved.

"Are they celebrating anything special?" she asked.

"No, nothing special; just a dance," he said.

The village had suddenly grown quiet. Lombe's mother moved about the compound busying herself with the preparation of a meal. Sandra watched her with curiosity and wonder. She was so calm and composed in her excitement.

"Sande," she called out loud, "I told you to sweep this place — now visitors have found us with all this dirt. You shame me."

Lombe translated. Sandra looked at Chaudry and laughed quietly.

"Mothers are so much alike everywhere," she said.

"It's so nice and peaceful here," he said.

"We always think so of our homes, don't we?" said Lombe.

"I suppose so," said Chaudry. "But there is something deep and peaceful about country people, don't you think?"

"I wonder," said Lombe. "Things can be harsh here."

"What do you mean?" Sandra asked.

"Well, the same cruelty that one meets in the towns one meets here. The same love; only it is expressed differently and . . ." He stopped.

"And what?" she asked eagerly.

"It is sort of shared — everyone takes part of it and therefore adds to the whole."

62

They sat quiet and thought about what Lombe had said.

"You sound very typical, Lombe," Chaudry said.

"Why?" he asked.

"I have never met an African in town who does not feel nostalgic about the country — and yet many of them would rather stay in the town and go to the Astronaut."

"You are exaggerating, Chaudry," she said.

"Am I, Lombe?" he asked.

"I don't know — but the town does trap one. It is an eternal sentence for many of us and we accept it — why, I don't know."

Lombe's mother brought in the food and left them to eat it. Outside the drums had begun and the fires began to light the bare place where the dance was to take place.

The dance picked itself up from broken pieces of china to build up to some tremendous whole. Almost like a symphony orchestra at rehearsal. Then the chorus shuffled itself around with the major vocalist trying to find the voice and the support. A girl wailed pleadingly a tune. A half-hearted refrain came back — she was not satisfied. One of the drums tried to push the whole along with a determined burst of thuds. They passed by, with the drum fading into bits and pieces of technical hand manoeuvres on the skin. Burning leaves were brought to warm the tops of the drums. The drums were tried again and found sound. Then the dance was on.

On it went, gathering pitch, momentum and fire. Drums. Drums, dancer and chorus all engulfed in one act of prayer. All forced to one act of submission. The drummers settled into a rhythm, each drum speaking to the other — encouraging, teasing, appealing, rising to a frenzied refusal to simply fit in with the others, defiance. Dancers leapt into the arena as if possessed by a grip that they could not shake off. Sweat poured down the bodies of the drummers. They glistened in the light of the fire, eyes closed, listening only to the harmony, their hands a maze of rhythm.

A lone voice from the crowd started a piercing refrain. It floated on top of the drums, lingering on, frightening and all by itself. Timidly, the crowd answered back. The voice pleaded again, this time to the crowd and to the drummers. The crowd reached for it and brought it down to the drummers and to itself. Suddenly, from the black corner of the crowd, a tall, dark woman came into the arena. She ran around it once stopping here and there to wriggle. She lay bare her bosom. Her breasts were hard and young. Her body supple and nimble. She stretched her hands to the drums and pleaded to them to take her.

She danced on solo for what seemed a long time. The crowd sang and clapped her on to the final act of submission. As she collapsed tired on the ground, the crowd started to dance. Each man and woman dancing by themselves but all dancing together. Where Chaudry, Sandra and Lombe sat, the magic of the dance burst the web of sophistication.

Sandra sat quiet and mesmerized. She had come to see a savage dance such as only Hollywood can put on the screen. A dance where men became beasts — savage beasts. One that would curdle the blood. Where men would foam at the mouth and fall down in fits. This was not the dance she saw tonight. Such dances were rare and could only be performed and seen on special occasions and by the initiates alone. There was savagery in the way the whole thing appealed to the core of one's being. It tore one from the roots and involved one bodily and spiritually. It was not a mere spectacle and the animal qualities in it were the

animal qualities that man shares with all the other created
things. It was the flight of the flamingo and the swallow.
The leap of the impala and the trudge of the buffalo. The
slither of the snake and the act of creation. The proud walk
of the giraffe. The kingly prowl of the lion.

The warm glow of the fire mixed with the sweat of
the dancing bodies. Movement glowed, shone and slithered
within itself and the glow of the fires. The drums mingled
with the refrain each holding the other and reaching to that
height that cannot be passed. Like waiting for a bomb to
explode — like that moment of eternity in the act of creation
when the after and the before are held in balance giving
the understanding of the mystery of life. It was impossible
to sit still. To sit and watch creation and not be part of it.
Lombe stood up. Chaudry and Sandra watched him. He
looked different. He shone as he took off his jacket and
tie, loosened the buttons of his collar and started to dance
with the crowd.

The crowd did not look at Lombe dancing. It felt him in
its midst like the way a lover feels the presence of his
beloved even in a crowded room. At each turn man turned
to the woman of his choice to marry the dance with. Then
they would dance to each other and then part to meet again
at a later stage. Lombe danced until his shirt dripped with
sweat. He was dancing months of emptiness and he felt
his life once again charged wth new strength. At the
Astronaut one lost strength in the dance, here one gained
strength in it.

The dance was now at that stage where it had to come
to an end. Lombe felt the touch of a familiar body. A
definite touch of a wet, warm body. It was a familiar
touch — like when in the stillness of thought one hears the
distinct call of one's name by someone one loves. A cold
numbness shook his body. Turning sideways to see what

that touch was, he saw the serene shadow of Miria dancing away from him with a faraway gaze that belonged to her life only. Lombe tried to reach for her but she was gone and lost in the crowd and the dance.

11

"You really must be careful, Lombe." This was Sammy well underway with drinks. His shirt was more than worse for wear. He badly needed a bath and a hair-cut.

"A new Cortina, already in the garage for panel beating." The crowd turned around, then burst into loud laughter.

"Not to worry — have another drink."

Lombe reached out for a glass of beer. His hands were visibly trembling. He gulped down half of it with a feeling of extreme gratitude.

"Tell us about the escapade with the Indian dame," demanded Brute. "You lucky bastard, what did you give in exchange?"

"I could give anything to fumble into those gorgeous saris," said Sammy.

"Tell you what," said Brute, "—let's make a deal with Lombe."

"Go ahead — I'm all for a deal with Lombe," Sammy chipped in.

"Tonight when we go to the Honourable with the goods — why don't we talk him into phoning the Indian brother to ask him to come over — with the kid, of course."

"Brilliant idea — how about it, Lombe?"

"Yes, man," taunted Sammy, "and that Moira piece as well."

"Time I think — we've been handing over our sisters to the whites at what I consider to be uneconomic returns — foreign aid and all that."

They all gleefully burst into laughter at what they thought was a great joke. Lombe fidgeted in his seat. He said, "I shall not be a party to your suggestion."

"What, man," said Sammy, "are you going to play the gentleman on us now that you revolve in high society?"

"Maybe he wants them all to himself," Brute said.

"Remember, man — we all have to pay the national debt."

Lombe felt his gorge rise in him. The anger was more sharpened by the vision of Miria at the dance. It cut like the edge of a barber's razor. He remembered the serene face of Sandra as they drove back — happy and contented. A vision of harmony but bearing a fire within that stirred other fires in Lombe which he had never dared to disturb. The savage, uncoordinated demands of Moira revolted him.

"Come on, man — speak up, why so quiet?" Sammy cajoled. "Or have you been so scared of the white queen that your thing couldn't stir?"

More beer was ordered. The fat girl brought it, wriggling like a fat worm after a meal. She brushed the back patch of her thigh against Lombe.

"Cold or warm for you, Mr. Lombe?"

"Cold, please."

"Do you remember the story of that young clerk on whom an Irish Secretary was mad?" inquired Brute of everyone around.

"No, Brute — tell us."

"Well, she was so gone on this lad — but the poor lad was so scared, so he went to a drunkard ex-mayor who specialized in Astronaut types for advice."

"And did the mayor oblige?"

"Yah," slowly replied Brute, building up for effect, "look my boy," said the old man, "they think you are all prolific and that you have yards of it. Pick up the phone and tell her — Baby, I'm coming to screw you hard tonight."

Peals of drunken laughter burst round the room.

"Cheers everybody. That's what they say, isn't it? Cheers, Lombe."

*　　　　　*　　　　　*

The Hon. Minister of Labour was at home that evening at his Permanent Secretary's house. It would not do to be at home at his own house with the wife there and all the kids. Konza, the Permanent Secretary, knew his Minister well. When Sammy's party arrived the Hon. Minister had already been safely enthroned in his favourite corner. His slippered feet were well propped up on a side table, a generous glass of brandy and ginger firmly and lovingly clasped in sausage fingers. His peals of glee burst out of his oversized tummy, held together by a T shirt.

"Good evening, sir," each repeated in mock reverence.

"Come in, boys — good to see you. Give the boys a drink, Konza."

The party sat down and worshipped.

"That was a magnificent speech you gave in Parliament yesterday, Minister."

"Oh! ho! did you think so?"

"It was very good, sir."

"Brute says it's the best he has heard you give."

The Hon. Minister of Labour looked shy and burst into a giggle of pride. He felt warm all over. The brandy had given him a glow of well-being. It had made him forget the order he had given to his henchmen in his constituency to go and beat up his opponent for daring to hold a meeting at which his name was mentioned.

"That looks like Mr. Lombe over there," the Minister said.

"Yes, sir."

"I thought so — I haven't got my glasses."

"I have just joined your Ministry, sir."

"Yes, I know. We need bright boys like you in the civil service. Leave politics to buffoons like us, eh!"

"I would not say that, sir."

"Well, I have heard very good reports about you."

"Thank you, sir."

"Yes — Konza — I want to see Mr. Lombe in my office tomorrow."

"Definitely, Minister, definitely."

Sammy crossed over to the radiogram. He put on a record as Mrs. Konza and her teenage daughter brought in more bottles of drink and assorted foods. The record ground to a stop as a large car also ground to a screeching stop outside. There was a chorus of teenage giggles as stilettos tapped their way in, wafted by cheap Indian scent.

The air in the room was full of tension as the driver opened the door to let company in.

It was the gang that Lombe first met at the diplomatic night. The large nurse, well strapped in an aluminium dress which, on catching the light, showed off all the curves of her body. Over her shoulders she had draped an old fur — very definitely picked up at the second-hand goods shop. The major feature of her face were the lips.

They looked as if one had been vamping a cow — almost an apparition of blood. It was difficult to see her eyes behind the dark and green coating of eye shadow. She tripped in, swaying her bottom — a smile frozen on her face like a marionette who knows the importance of performance. Of the group she looked the most prosperous. The others were indifferent. Divided between the coarse from hostels, the Mercedes Benz impressed, and the Astronaut types.

Sammy and Brute made them comfortable on the sofa.

"What's yours, Bettie?" asked Brute of the large nurse. She wriggled slightly in her chair looking at Minister Chozo, at the same time trying to pull down her dress over her thighs.

"Whisky and beer, please," she said calmly.

"It shall be done, baby." And so it was done by Sammy, as best as he only could do it. Round the room the liquor flowed and everyone began to relax.

It was about midnight when the phone rang. Sammy answered it — then midway turned to Lombe and said, "For you," with a rather mischievous grin.

Lombe looked startled. He had never received a telephone call outside office hours in his life. Least of all at midnight and at the Permanent Secretary's house. He walked over, his feet rather unsteady and one of the girls clinging precariously on his shoulder. He picked up the receiver and put the mouth end to his ear. All he could hear were strong heaves of breath from the other end. He looked enquiringly at the girl on his arm. She giggled and turned the phone the right way. He gave her a peck kiss on the nose.

"Hello — Lombe speaking."

"Hello darling — Moira here."

Silence. "Who is speaking?"

"Moira — you do remember me?"

"Yes."

"I just wanted to say hello to you and ask you whether you are enjoying the party!"

"Oh, yes — very much indeed, madam."

"Shit!" came the distraught voice from the other end.

"What did you say?"

"I said I'll phone you again tomorrow."

"Tomorrow." His eyes lit as he remembered a particular sentence rather vividly. He breathed hard into the phone and said, "Yes, tomorrow screwing tight!"

He dropped the phone on its rest and gave a hysterical laugh that sent them both rolling on the carpet. After some difficulties of managing themselves up they noticed that the room was empty.

"Where is everyone?" he asked.

"I think they have gone somewhere."

"Where?"

"I don't know," she said, with a mischievous look in her eyes.

"What shall we do?"

"I don't know." He screwed his face to impress the little girl.

With great emotion she took him by the hand and said, "Let's go to my house."

"O. K."

12

"Aren't you going to wake up?"

She shook him vigorously — roughly off the bed. Lombe groaned and tried to reach for her.

"Take your hands off me, I must go to work. Are you not going to the office?" she stabbed sharply.

Lombe shook himself from his stupor of sleep and drink. He looked about him. The room looked odd.

"Where am I?" he muttered to himself.

"Get up — I must go to work!"

It was a low room with a low tin roof. He was lying on a short, wooden bed. His limbs were aching from the bulges of a well-beaten, cotton mattress. The only ventilation was a small window well up on the side of the wall. It had never been opened since the architect and builder finished this remarkable dwelling. There was a strong smell of beer, paraffin, stale air and sex. It was damp. In the gloom of the light which penetrated through the window Lombe saw, on the wall, old dresses and dirty underclothes hanging on nails. Two pairs of shoes stood on a petrol box. In the corner a paraffin stove and near it an old bunch of green bananas.

She was sitting on the side of the bed dressed in tattered Japanese underwear. Her breasts hung loosely down her chest. They were all crumpled and flat. Her thighs were full of scabs. She looked at him with an amused, doleful air. He had not undressed. He lay on the bed, fully clothed, with his shoes on — his legs dangling in the air at the other end of the bed. Where his head was, lay a greasy lump of sweat and grime which passed for a pillow. His mouth was bitter and stale. Sweat and stale air pricked his body.

"Get up — I must go," she snapped.

Lombe suddenly realized where he was.

"You certainly are in a foul mood today."

"I am late for work — please get up," she said.

He watched her put on her best clean dress over the dirty mess of underclothes. She pulled on a pair of cheap stockings over her legs — reached for a comb and brush — smeared the secrets of South African cosmetics on her face and presto! — the image that had dragged Lombe to bed the previous night returned to remind him what had happened to him. Lombe felt sick. He felt rotten and filthy, both inside and outside.

"Can I have some water to wash?"

"You will find water in that bucket over there."

"Where is the washing place?"

"You can use the basin or go outside."

She fumbled with her keys — impatiently. Lombe tried hard to remember the name of the girl. It was impossible. She was many names and many faces.

Outside he heard the sound of men on bicycles going to work. Women passed and handed jokes in loud voices using vulgar colourful language. He could distinctly hear someone piss against the wall outside. A strong, hot jet that sizzled cold in the morning air. A child was crying somewhere nearby and no one paid attention to its cries. What was the name of this girl? He had seen her on occasions at the Astronaut and at one time remembered that he had been very rude to her; in company with Miria, he had used foul language on her when she asked for a light for her cigarette.

Lombe levered himself up. His shoes were muddy, his jacket and trousers were full of creases. His tie had twisted itself into a screw-driver; and he smelt. He smelt of her, her bed, her room and of the whole surroundings of this famous slum.

Then fright took him. He must get out of this place quickly. He must get away before it was too light. He could not afford to be seen and recognized by anyone who knew him, coming out of this house and this slum and at that time of the day.

"My God!" he muttered.

"What time is it?"

"You have a watch — haven't you — I can't afford one." He looked at his wrist. The watch was not there.

"Where did I put my watch?"

"Did you give it to me?"

"But I had it on last night."

"Then you must have it."

"Don't play tricks with me."

"You can search the room if you wish," she said.

Lombe suddenly felt a spasm of fear. He fumbled in the pockets of his trousers, there was nothing. He reached into the pockets of his jacket. There was no watch.

"My w . . .," he began.

"Now don't say you can't find it," she said with an injured look.

"My wallet — where is my wallet?" he asked desperately.

"Your what?" she asked calmly.

"My wallet," he added loudly.

"You come to my house, dead drunk. I keep you and now you want to accuse me of stealing your watch and your money."

"No, I didn't say that — perhaps it has fallen down."

"Why don't you look?" she said. She fumed and fussed round the room making it clear that her services must be paid for before he left.

"I wish I had not had the decency to look after you — do you think I live on nothing?" She began to raise her voice at each word.

"You call yourself a gentleman — gentleman indeed." She reached for her best pair of shoes and then turned round looking at him accusingly.

"I really had them on me last night," he mumbled, beads of sweat forming on his forehead.

"You saw me with them, didn't you?" he appealed to her. He was feeling prickly all over. He thought that the only way of breaking her down was to appeal to her good nature. There must be some soft core somewhere in this tough child of the slums. All the money he had to see him through the month was in that wallet. He had expected to pay off a few Indian debts this month. Already they had refused to give him goods on credit. The wallet must be somewhere in this room.

He jumped off the bed and, like a maniac, turned over every single bit of it. He crept underneath the bed and pulled away from this underworld all the dirt that slum beds store. A pair of tattered men's shoes. An old umbrella, cooking pots — a man's pair of pants — all caked with old blood. When he emerged, trembling and hot, from under the bed, the girl was standing looking at him with an amused smile on her face. Lombe looked at her and said, "It is not there."

The girl looked at him, lit a cheap half bit of cigarette and burst out into a mocking giggle.

"I have heard your story before, Mr. Lombe," she said. "I am not a child."

"Please do believe me," he pleaded.

The light in the window cracks was getting stronger. Streaming in and criss-crossing jet lines of white on the walls. He looked about him — helpless and silly in his now dusty suit.

"Please believe me!" he pleaded. She just looked at him.

"Come to my office — I'll give you your money." She looked at him.

"Come to the Astronaut tonight — I shall have money then — please don't shout." She looked at him. There was a knock on the door. Lombe froze where he stood.

"Kristine! Kristine! are you in?" It was a female voice.

"Kristine —aren't you going to work today?"

"I am coming," she said.

Her footsteps walked away in the cold morning. Lombe flung himself at the wooden door — wrenched it open and out like a mad person, through the grime-filled channels of the slum sewerage system.

13

It was a cold day. One which blew the cold mists that made office rooms miserable. A patch of wet greyness spread on the ceiling. But the walls were solid — reflecting the mentality of those that built them. Colonial fortresses that were built to reflect authority and permanency. The office furniture was hard solid wood reminiscent of Eton classroom desks. With progress came grey metal filing cabinets trying very hard to preserve the feeling of power and dignity in their torpid greyness. A khaki clad whiteman was the only piece of furniture lacking in the shrine of this past era.

Lombe remembered with a shudder the morning, a number of years ago, when as a boy an Askari had pushed him into the den of power. The priest was very young. He carried his blond hair with the pride of a lion. Burning red and fiery behind the huge *muvule* table behind which Lombe now sat. The room had then looked immensely big. He had felt so small and lonely in it. He had come to ask for money to pay for his fees at a distant secondary school. All these things one had been told could be got at the Boma. The Boma was a magic shrine where the white priests performed the wonders that had subdued the black man. The white young man had greeted him with a growl of his mother tongue distilling from it all the sweetness that he had come to respect in it. When asked what his name was Lombe could not remember it.

The telephone rang — a long incessant ring that brought him back to the present. His fingers were trembling as he picked up the receiver. His mind was a conglomeration of myriad thoughts and fears. For the first time since occupying this office Lombe was scared of the phone. Was it the Secretary wishing to see him? Could it after all be the girl? Or was it Patel after his money? He picked up the receiver and in great pain managed to whisper into it — "Lombe speaking."

"Lombe speaking."

"Mr. Lombe," cooed the receptionist. "A lady wishes to speak to you — shall I put her on?"

"A lady?" repeated Lombe.

"Yes, Mr. Lombe — a lady."

There was silence on the line as the girl waited and Lombe tried hard to sound casual and think out a way of finding out from her who this lady was. She did not give him time.

"Shall I put her on, Mr. Lombe?"

There was no escape. He had to go through with it.

"Yes, please — put her on," he muttered.

"Hello, Mr. Lombe," cracked through a cheery and rather loud voice. Lombe put the receiver a few inches from his ear. It was not an African voice. He could however hear the echoes of this particular voice several drunken evenings ago.

He could now smell the mascara in it and the creams that make up a face to go to bed.

"Hello," he said — pretending not to know.

"Who is speaking?"

"Oh you bum — can't you remember? Moira," the phone said from the other end. She had said she would phone him just to say hello.

"Hello, Miss Moira," he said in his confusion. What did one say to a person one hardly knew except for one evening in her bed. A week ago Lombe had no phone and shared an office. Life had been occasionally dull but he had never felt so trapped. The few ticks of silence made him miserable. The crack came through again this time with a rather injured roll of a cigarette-holder.

"I just wanted to keep my promise — am I disturbing you?"

"No, not really. I was just about to ring you myself," he lied.

"Well — how are you?" she asked.

"Very well indeed — how about you."

"You are very naughty you know," she said.

"Why?" he asked.

"You know why — why didn't you say goodbye before you left the party."

Lombe had a good reason why he did not say goodbye before he left. He was afraid to tell her why. This was the first time in his life that he had ever been seduced by a woman. He had not quite fully understood why this white woman had picked on him. So many stories were going around town these days that the white woman had gone amock over black men. To be seen with one was a source of endless teasing from friends. The white goddess had been freed from her white shrine and was now busy eating the forbidden fruit wherever she could find it. Worse still, the stories said that the white man had also rebelled from the white woman and was making havoc with black schoolboys.

"Are you still there?" she asked.

"Yes — I'm sorry, someone has just walked into my office — I'll ring you later."

"Alright — don't forget — my number is 56743." As an urgent afterthought she added, "I love you — see you soon."

She put down the telephone with the full advantage of striking the blow from which recovery needs time. Lombe looked at the receiver oozing with the breath of animal desire. His hand shook. He put the receiver down only to start it again on another ringing spree. Feeling certain that this was an official call, he braced himself and shouted a firm hello into the receiver.

"Another lady for you, Mr. Lombe."

"Good God!" gasped Lombe.

Before he could collect his thoughts the receptionist had put the caller through.

"Hello, Jonathan." It was a soft warm voice.

"Hello — who is speaking?" Before he had asked the question he knew who the person was. Excitement welled up in him. Was it possible?

"Sandra — Chaudry's sister — remember?" Of course he remembered and felt stupid at having played the game of telephones.

"Yes, of course I do — I..."

She cut him short. "I'm sorry to call you at the office."

"That is quite alright — I have not yet put a phone in my house." The second half was added for impression.

"Are you very busy this evening?" she asked in a matter of fact manner.

"Yes — I mean NO," he shouted back.

"Oh — good, then you must come to a surprise birthday party we are having for Chaudry."

"A party?" he muttered back foolishly.

"Yes, a party for Chaudry — can you come?" she asked with a plea in her voice.

"Yes, thank you Miss Sandra."

He cursed himself for getting caught up with 'Miss' and 'Sir' each time he spoke to these people.

"That's wonderful," she said. "See you at eight-thirty — good-bye."

She rang off almost immediately after the good-bye. Lombe lamely repeated the good-bye into a cold receiver. He had never pretended to understand foreigners. His association with Europeans had been formal and correct. He had known this ever since he was at school. One did not only have to pass examinations but also be what the white teachers called polite. The same formula had served him as a junior civil servant. By the time independence was approaching he had broken away from this servile formula but kept the white man away by creating a bridge between himself and them, fortified by meaningless smiles — and seemingly agreeing with everything they said. The Indian world had been closed for him. There was no need even to make a gesture. And now into his life had walked this Indian mystery.

He was fascinated by Sandra. He did not see a woman in her. He saw some kind of meaning — some kind of inner light — a shaft of inward peace that he had never experienced before. This was the peep hole into the shadow of Indians he had passed by every day of his life on the pavements of the city. Impassive, quiet, serious and unconcerned. Suddenly he felt terror well up in him as he tried to picture Sandra. In many ways she had so much in common with Miria. Miria, the village girl who in spite of her crudity possessed a soul that penetrated every curvature of his patched up humanity. A humanity of patched up values of so many unknown cultures. The phone rang.

"Mr. Lombe, an Indian gentleman to see you."

Could this be Chaudry? he wondered. He quickly rearranged his table to give it a look of being busy and asked the receptionist to show the Indian gentleman in. Lombe set in the motion of fumbling with files. He put a lot of files marked 'Confidential' in front of him. They looked impressive and gave the impression of competence. The messenger knocked on the door.

"Come in," he shouted with the voice of a sergeant major at a parade ground.

"Mr. Gupta Afendi," saluted the messenger. He too had to take his chance for pomposity. Mr. Gupta walked in. A short grey-haired Indian. He was dressed in dirty blue overalls. Gupta was the local mechanic in town who between selling second hand cars to low salaried civil servants and low income business men made his fortune by keeping them off and on the road. This he did by putting back in faulty spare parts. Lombe became excited at seeing him in his office. Usually he only came to offices to collect bad debts. Lombe pointed him to a seat.

"Mr. Lombe, Sir," he began with an oily smile on his face. This smile was part of Gupta's mask. He wore it every time he talked to anyone. "So wery good dat you can see me — I come wit wery good news — yes."

"Good morning, Mr. Gupta — have a seat."

"Oh tank you, Mr. Lombe, sir." Gupta looked around with assumed interest and added, "Dis you have here is a wery good big office — no!"

"Not very big really — have a seat."

"Oh! tank you wery much — but I can stand also, Mr. Lombe sir." Gupta sat down.

"What can I do for you Mr. Gupta? I haven't got much time this morning."

Gupta ignored the remark. He had heard it many times and knew it was part of a civil service greeting.

"Yes Mr. Lombe sir, as I say to my prends — Independence wery good ting." He thought he had said some profound thing and laughed nervously.

"Look now," he added. "I come to office where I no come bepore." Gupta threw his hands in the air and kneaded and sawed with dainty fingers as he uttered these words of patriotism.

"I am glad you like the office, Mr. Gupta — is there anything I can do for you — I have to see the Minister in a few minutes." More as a threat and as one of those pieces of civil service vocabulary.

"Of course yes Mr. Lombe sir, wery rude of me — please excuse. I come only por little matter you know." Lombe tried to find the truth with a question.

"Is the car ready?"

"Perfectly and I tought I must bring him here myself to you." This announcement he made with utter joy. Lombe braced himself for what was to come next. Was Gupta going to ask for cash? Maybe he could play for time by offering a post dated cheque. He had given four of them already and these almost covered this month's salary.

"You vant to come and see him, Mr. Lombe?" asked Gupta with a twinkle in his eye.

"You cannot see he had an accident — perfectly Mr. Lombe." Lombe got stuck for words.

"I know vat you tinking Mr. Lombe — you tink I vant money now." Gupta assumed the posture of Bhuda and in a solemn voice said. "Sometimes business is business — sometime a prend is a prend, acha." Lombe felt stupified by this declaration.

87

"How much is it going to cost?" he asked.

"Por you Mr. Lombe — I make only one hundred and pipty pound." Gupta waited for the shaft to find its mark. He could see that Lombe was definitely becoming uncomfortable. This is what he had expected. The web had been set the previous evening at Patel's over a game of cards. Patel had threatened to sue Lombe for a post dated cheque which had now become stale. Gupta kept it in his heart and he was now going to use it to swing his deal.

"One hundred and fifty pounds," muttered Lombe.

"I make it wery cheap por you Mr. Lombe — another garage of these swindlers in town Mr. Lombe would have asked much more dan dis — but it is a wery small matter please — as I say bepore a prend is a prend and a prend must help a prend also."

"I understand and appreciate it very much."

"Don't say dat Mr. Lombe sir. In fact I come to tell you por dis job I make pree por you as prend."

"Free," exclaimed Lombe with surprise.

"Pree — absolutely pree."

"But why, Mr. Gupta?"

Gupta looked at Lombe with a hurt expression on his face. He had never met such a naive young person before. Pity that he had to use him. These educated ones were really raw. He had expected this question and had prepared the only answer that could shatter the kind of pride that goes with these young men who did not understand the basic laws of business.

"You ask me vy Mr. Lombe?" he said with a quiver of hurt anger. "No matter den — ip you tink dat I do wrong please porget — excuse me I only vanted to do as prend." Gupta said this with much pain in his voice.

"I did not mean that, Mr. Gupta — please don't misunderstand me."

"Not to vory Mr. Lombe — perhaps I do wrong — you see."

"No, no, I am most grateful to you, Mr. Gupta — it is a great relief to me I can assure you."

"Alright den — put it dis way Mr. Lombe — you pay ven you can — today — tomorrow — next year or in heaven." Gupta laughed out loud at what he thought was an excellent joke. It worked. The tension eased. Gupta knew that he had won half the battle.

"Only sign receipt Mr. Lombe and den porget matter por now if you like — dis I ask as prend." Lombe had not expected this windfall. He knew that he should not accept this offer. He knew that there must be a trick somewhere. But either way the choice was bound. After all, this was business between him and a businessman. Naturally Gupta wanted to capture him as a regular customer. Maybe also use him to get some of his friends who were now buying cars every day to be his customers. There was nothing wrong in this. He felt he had to show some warmth to the Indian.

"And how is business these days, Mr. Gupta?"

"Oh! say pipty pipty Mr. Lombe sir." He waved the fifty fifty in his hand with the delicacy of balancing scales.

"Van day good van day bad — hacha! But I must go now Mr. Lombe I take too much of your waluable time." Gupta made as if to move.

"But I must say how very th...."

"Don't say it again Mr. Lombe — de happiness is mine only — hacha." Gupta stood up and took two steps towards the door then turned back sharply like one who has forgotten something trivial behind.

"Oh! just one ting Mr. Lombe — small matter I porgot to ask you for adwice only as prend."

"Yes, Mr. Gupta. Anything I can help."

"Not much really Mr. Lombe — but you might give me paherps adwice only."

"Yes."

"Vel — you see," he said with his head sorrowfully inclined on one side.

"Vel I received dis letter prom your office on a little matter — you know." Gupta fumbled in his pockets and took out a brown official envelope. Lombe reached for the letter. Gupta fixed him with a pleading look. He watched him as he read it. It was from the Ministry signed by the Chief Inspector of Factories.

"This is a serious matter Mr. Gupta," Lombe tried to avoid Gupta's gaze as he said this.

"Mr. Lombe sir, I explained to this gentleman that I pix all dis by dis month — truth God Mr. Lombe — you know how dis kind ting take time to pix." It was a sad story and Lombe could not help but sympathise.

In a doleful voice he said, "But the matter has now gone to court, Mr. Gupta."

"How you expect me ignorant to know dat, Mr. Lombe sir?" Lombe had clearly to do something. He knew what to do. He could have done it minutes ago before he signed receipts for repair of a car involved in an unreported accident.

"Vel Mr. Lombe sir," added Gupta with the lameness of an injured friend. "I just vanted your adwice — as prend." The net was around Lombe. The one thing he had to do at this moment he hesitated to do.

"Wait a moment," he said. "Leave the letter with me — I'll see what I can do — but I do not promise much Mr. Gupta."

"I know you are prend Mr. Lombe sir. I know you can help prend Mr. Lombe. God help you Mr. Lombe sir — hacha!" With unending genuflections Gupta slipped out of his office and out into the world he knew so well. Lombe

90

was left with the letter in his hands. Each time he looked at it, it increased in weight. And so it was until it fell on the table with the lightness of paper but the weight of lead.

*   *   *

It was a day of telephones. An hour after Gupta's departure the phone rang again. On that wet and gloomy morning the ring of the telephone had an ominous sound. He picked the receiver and gave that stupid reply that every civil servant says into a telephone.

"Hello — extension 678 Lombe speaking."

"Mr. Lombe could you please come to my office at once." It was the voice of the Permanent Secretary.

"Yes, sir."

Lombe stuffed Gupta's letter in his pocket. He had never been summoned to the Perm. Sec's. office by the PS himself. This must be important. He began to wonder what the matter was. Had someone laid a trap for him through Gupta? Was it the girl? The Perm. Sec. received him with more cordiality than usual.

"Have a seat, Mr. Lombe — the Minister wants to see you."

Kango was one of those solid people that had made themselves. He was dependable. Having finished school at junior secondary level he had worked systematically for a university degree by correspondence. He had set his sights and attained his goal at the age of forty. He would have liked to do more. He would have liked to get into politics for instance and become a Minister. He knew he could do better than most. But his ambition to get to the top in his studies and the civil service had made him cautious. When the time came to make the move he had been caught by a rather stupid woman whom he had married. When he became PS she got fatter and produced more children for him. Kango had now to resign himself to a job he knew he would hold for the better part of his life and a Mercedes Benz. But his subordinates liked him because he was fair and liked to be liked. He also enjoyed the aura of being important in the way that a bureaucracy makes one imagine its importance because otherwise it would not work — or grind on, as it painfully does. Public service it is called in respectable circles.

"Excuse me, sir, do you know why he wants to see me?" Kango did not want to admit that he did not know. But he was so honest that he could not give an answer. So he put on a conspiratorial clumsy smile and said, "I'll go and see if he is ready for you."

Lombe was ushered into the Minister's office as soon as Kango had poked his head through the door. The Minister of Labour was fumbling with the phone importantly as Lombe entered. He barked into the telephone and swivelled his big bellied self around. Unfortunately the voice on the other side was so loud that it came through the receiver with a cracking punch. It could not be mistaken. It was the voice of the fat nurse.

"I am sorry I am in conference now," Chozo said importantly. "I have given instructions to my personal secretary to phone you and put you in the picture." The receiver was then laid down with an air of the cares of the world temporarily cut off.

"Some of these people do not think that we have any work to do here except listen to their mad projects." The Minister received the sympathy and understanding that he expected.

"I don't think I'll need you, Mr. Kango."

"Very well, Minister." Kango shuffled out of the room, his hands held in prayer in front of him. Lombe was asked to sit down.

"Thank you, sir" he said, breathlessly.

The Minister looked at the young man for some time. Then he broke into a sly piggy laugh.

"You are a smart fellow Lombe — I like you." The remark took Lombe by surprise. He did not know what to say.

"You see," continued the Minister, "some of you young men don't know how much we do for you. You think that because you are educated you should jump all the steps that we old politicians have created for you."

This was beyond Lombe's comprehension.

"I'm very happy in my job, sir," he mumbled. Chozo dismissed the interjection with disgust. He knew he was handling a kid from sap. "I shall be going on a tour of the West region next week — I want you to come with me as my personal secretary."

Chozo watched Lombe as he wriggled with surprise and excitement.

"It is a great honour, sir."

"It is nothing, Lombe — you deserve it," he said. Then as man to man he added, "Kango is a good man but very old fashioned."

They laughed. Chozo because he meant it. Lombe because it flattered him. Chozo flashed a fatherly smile at Lombe.

"By the way that was a lovely party — did you enjoy it?"

"Yes, sir, very much."

"Good, I am glad to hear it — you see man must relax sometimes," Chozo gave Lombe a knowing wink. Lombe giggled to release the tension.

"Do you know that Indian girl well?" he asked as an afterthought. Lombe was stuck for an answer. "And her brother well?"

"Fairly well, sir," he said — uncertain of what he meant.

Chozo put on his fatherly smile again and said, "Jonathan — as man to man, because I like you very much, can you do a small thing for me?"

"Yes, sir — I'd feel most honoured."

"Make a fixture soon eh? Use my account at Patel's for anything you will require," he said firmly.

"A fixture, sir!" exclaimed Lombe.

"Don't pretend so much." He laughed out loudly.

"Somewhere nice and quiet — eh! and get ready for the trip to the west."

"Yes, sir."

"Ask Kango to come in, will you."

The corridors of the Ministry were full of clerks and secretaries as Lombe walked out of the Minister's office. Religiously at the strike of the gong the junior officers fled to their homes like smoked rats. Lombe joined them, his mind full of one odd sentence, "Make a fixture."

14

The government bungalow where Lombe lived began
to show signs of missing its mistress. Miria had kept the
floors clean. She had a fine hand for tidying things.
The house was her secret pride. In it she had expressed
silently the love and pride she had for Lombe. She had often
said to herself that it was impossible to converse with
Lombe. He had too many big ideas about love, justice and
similar heavy-handed subjects. So she put all her words
into action. Whenever she had him to herself she slaved
around him. He resented this sometimes but she knew
him so well that unless she wanted him to do something for
her she left him alone at such times.

Lombe had avoided the house as much as he could after
Miria had left. He did not want to go back and not find
Miria there, but also he did not want to find her there.
Somehow the present state of the house reflected the state
of his mind and life. The short grass in front of the house had

grown into bush. The floors had not been swept. Dirty crockery lay scattered around the room. The bed was perpetually unmade. The bedroom smelt of dirty sheets and stale air. A bundle of dirty socks and browned underwear lay in a pile in one corner. He looked at them in disgust, not for their dirtiness but that he had made them dirty. He had to change for this party. From the pile in the corner he selected the least dirty pair of socks. They were hard and starched on the soles. He decided not to change his shirt. He selected his best suit. He tried to smooth down the creases with a cold iron.

He was in a state of depression. Each time he walked around the house he saw visions of Miria. He had expected her to return to him. He was disappointed that she had not come back. A sense of shame and guilt overtook him because he had not made enquiries about her. He was annoyed that she had not even bothered to come and talk to him when he took Chaudry and Sandra to his home. He could not forget the way she had danced. Seemingly giving herself away to the gods and cleansing herself from him and all his type in the cities where people went to die. His sense of pride gnawed with disappointment that she had not come back to him on her knees. He looked for the bottle of gin that he kept in the room. It was very low. Soon he would have to buy another one. He could not manage to face the world sober. The effort to appear calm and efficient; to carry on the day to day bits of living with his friends, Sammy, Brute and the others, had drained him to a point where he knew a breakdown was near. The effort to make himself not believe that it was near drained him out more. Occasionally he caught himself giving odd twitches of the hand as he wrote. That is why he looked forward to going to Sandra. Sandra was the kind of woman that

he had wanted Miria to be. Handsome, motherly and
sophisticated in the ways of the city. In her he saw Miria.
Above all somehow he felt he could be like a baby in her
presence. She charged his batteries. The loneliness around
him now was too oppressive. He took the gin and moved
into the other room. As he settled down to have a drink
there was a loud knock on the door. Lombe spilled the glass
of gin and looked like a frightened rabbit. The knock
came through again. Lombe wondered who this could be.
Definitely none of his friends. Could it be the girl or was
it Miria?

"Is anyone in?" a voice asked.

"Who is it?" Lombe asked.

"Oh, you are in — I want to talk to you."

Lombe went to the door and opened it slightly. He
knew the man. He had seen him several times before. Two
years ago he was the talk of the town. He had been
fabulously rich. For some reason or other the then colonial
government had given him contracts. People knew that he
acted as an informer to the police. So they called him "The
Stooge." The worst name that the country could call
anyone. It meant you did not only lick the whiteman's arse
but he used you to do his dirty work and asked you to
betray your own people. Easy money had given him that
colonial mentality that believed that the whiteman was there
forever and that all the other Africans who were shouting
for Independence were mad — crazy. Independence had
come. It had taken him by surprise like a whirlwind. At
first he had thought it a joke until his business was
hit by an official boycott. To be seen talking to him was
a crime. He was a kind of pox to the people. If you did
not run away from it, it would catch you and you would
slowly rot.

"What do you want?" asked Lombe.

"Can I come in for a short time."

"Say what you want here and go."

"Even when it concerns Miria?" he said. He put on a faint smile; it was a cunning mocking smile.

Lombe looked at either side of the road and then said sharply, "Come in."

He closed the door firmly. The other man took a chair near the window. It was a strategic point. He could be seen by people walking outside if he wanted to. But now he sat leaning away from the window. He spoke first.

"You are Mr. Lombe."

"My name is Lombe."

He looked at him with a feeling of satisfaction — taking his time. Lombe sat fidgeting and waiting for him to say what he wanted to say.

"You probably do not know me, Mr. Lombe."

"I have seen you on several occasions."

"Yes, you have seen me on several occasions but you do not know me."

He put on his smile again — stalking his man like a cat stalking a rat. Teasing it and twitching its tail before the final plunge. Lombe waited. It seemed a long time and a long wait. At no point in his life could he see any thread that could possibly knit their lives together. All he wanted at this moment was to be alone — with his thoughts and his worries.

"This is a fine house you got, Mr. Lombe," he said. Lombe did not reply.

"I am not surprised to hear that you don't know me — I am Miria's uncle."

The room reeled around Lombe.

"She never told me," he mumbled lamely.

"I am not surprised."

98

He pulled out a packet of cigarettes. A deliberate slow choice of a cigarette to make Lombe uncomfortable.

"You don't mind if I smoke?"

Lombe shook his head. The panic that he had felt began to leave him and impatient anger welled up in him. Should he throw this man out — should he just leave the house and go away?

"I am sorry you have found me about to go to an important engagement," he foiled.

"I know you are a very busy man, Mr. Lombe — I shall not keep you long." He pulled hard at his cigarette, inhaling the smoke with a cold hard hiss.

"Well, as you know, things have not been easy for me since Independence — I thought that now that you are a kind of member of the family I should come and ask for help from you."

"What do you mean?"

"As you know, I was misguided by those Europeans. What could I do? The name of Samba has now become a swear word. People call their dogs Samba — but don't forget that I played my part as well." He took a long drag at his cigarette looking very thoughtful. It is true that years back Samba had been a keen nationalist. But he had been too clever and had frightened the local party officials. The money from his business had been useful for the party until funds from sources abroad had made his usefulness unnecessary. The whispering campaign then started and Samba was thrown out of the party and branded a 'stooge' and 'sell out.' In a fit of rage he teamed up with a party started by a dyed-in-the-wool white liberal. They had flown him all over Europe. But the end for him had begun.

"What do you want to tell me?" Lombe asked firmly.

"I know what has happened between you and Miria."

He waited for the words to sink in. Lombe did not make a reply.

"I thought we should discuss it man to man. Put it this way Mr. Lombe, you are not a small boy and I do not wish in any way to harm you. If you can help me — I shall let the matter lie." Samba looked out of the window — a gesture which Lombe did not want him to make as he could easily be seen through it.

"You see," he continued. "When those enemies of mine ruined me they thought I could not rise again. But Samba is no fool — I have got them now and I need your help."

"What help can I give you?"

"I want to see the President."

"You want to see the President!"

"Yes, I want to see the President."

"And how do you expect me to take you to see the President?"

"You know your Minister well."

"I work for him."

"I did not mean that — I mean that you know him well personally. You go to parties together and do a lot of things together." He said the "together" with the thickness of a knowing tongue.

"I have very important documents with me which I want to show him."

"You know that I cannot do this."

"You can. I want you to introduce me privately to your Minister."

Lombe realised now that the trap was more serious than he had thought. Either way the consequences were enormous for him. If the introduction to the Minister did not work he would be jobless in no time. If he refused to do what Samba was asking there would follow a scandal that would destroy him completely. He had never

100

realised that the world carried on its lap such scraps of
evil as he had been meeting ever since he came into what
is called a position of influence. What he had to do was
to get rid of this man completely out of his life. Samba
saw the thoughts in Lombe's mind. He stood up and said,
"Think about it — I shall be back in two days time here —
same time, to hear from you."

As an afterthought he turned to Lombe and said, "By
the way, how is Miria?"

He did not wait for the answer which Lombe was
trying hard to produce.

*   *   *

As Sammy ground the gears of the car and came to a
showy stop in front of Lombe's house, he saw the old man
leaving.

"The Stooge" he breathed out through his teeth. "Was
that not 'The Stooge' coming out of Lombe's?"

"Christ," said Brute. "It was the pox himself."

They burst into Lombe's house.

"Hey man," demanded Sammy. "What is the meaning
of all this?"

"It was Samba," Lombe said.

"We know it was 'The Stooge' man — but what is the
meaning? Give us the story, man?"

"He is Miria's uncle."

"My God!" exclaimed Sammy.

"Come with us pronto to the Astronaut, man — this
is hot stuff. I don't want to catch the pox in here."

"What shall I do, people?"

"Do?" snapped out Brute. "Disinfect yourself quick —
don't you know that the whole country is full of hatching
plots of revolution and coups?"

"And you go and get yourself entangled with the
timebomb itself?"

"You must have lost your nut."

"Come on, let's blow."

"I can't," said Lombe.

"Why — what's up?"

"I am going to the Chaudrys — in fact I'm supposed to be there now."

Sammy and Brute looked at each other in disbelief.

"OK then, meet us after your High Society folk," said Sammy. The two got into the car and drove off. Lombe watched the dust rise after them and felt sick.

15

It was a good party. Chaudry was excited by the surprise. Sandra had picked the visitors well. Besides Minister Chozo there were his father and mother and a few assorted cousins and friends. Lombe was the only other African in the group.

"You see, Excellency," began Ambassador Chaudry, "this preoccupation about the Indian community keeping to itself is grossly overstated." He was a man of about fifty. Neatly dressed and well preserved. He had an academic face and an aristocratic bearing. He had taken the job for the ease of avoiding taking the decision to be involved in public politics in India. His friends had always been pushing him to fight for Parliament but he had resisted. Secretly he knew he had wasted much time and he was slowly becoming a failure to himself. It was too late at fifty to start on anything worthwhile. He was very ambitious for his two children and saw in them the fulfilment of his own long past desires. Sandra was his special love. But Sandra was a bit difficult. She had too many independent ideas of her own. He had felt hurt when he learned that she had visited an African village without his permission. He did not quite like the idea of her being associated with Chaudry's African friends. He must soon find some way of sending her back to India. He picked up his glass of coca cola and continued.

"You see, Excellency, the Indian here is very much an African. He is a native in the right sense of the word — you see he has been involved in a different way with the material change of the country, and this has been his major contribution to the struggle for Independence."

"You are quite correct, Mr. Ambassador," Chozo agreed with little enthusiasm. He had to say something. "But there is only one little thing that I do not understand about our Indian brothers and sisters."

"I know what you are going to say, Minister," chipped in the Ambassador. He had been explaining this little thing nearly every day in Africa and had grown tired of it. The irritation of plugging a line which he knew was stale and false always reminded him of his growing weakness and the decline of that honesty and conviction for which he was famed as a young man at the University and in public service.

"Why don't they mix more with the Africans — why don't they take citizenship quickly — why do they send all their money to India?"

"Precisely," said Chaudry with some heat and a glint in his eye. Chaudry had always found his father cold to talk to. His father found him rather impetuous and rather rash in his actions. In some ways it reminded him of his own youth when he had no time for tedious narrow-mindedness.

"Precisely," he repeated. "Do you really believe, father,

104

that the Indian here has ever been interested in anything but what he makes in business or the professions? He talks a lot of cant about Independence now but we all know that as far as he cares, so long as he is safe he will support the devil himself."

"Look at it this way, Daddy," came in Sandra with more heat. "The Indian has penetrated more into the African life than even the best missionaries and the best administrators. He has rubbed shoulders with the most traditional and primitive in the remotest corners of this country and yet has remained a world utterly and irrevocably apart."

"Indo-African children are entirely from Indian fathers and African mothers; that is the nearest it has come to, even after the man eaters of Tsavo and the sugar plantations of South Africa — even then the mothers of these products hardly knew or lived with the husband."

Chozo had paid little attention to this heated argument. Sandra had been burning fire into him ever since he arrived at the party. The conversation was tedious and he was getting impatient. The glow of the whisky and soda was beginning to rise to his heart. He could not keep his eyes off Sandra.

"Mr. Ambassador," he said. "These young people I am sure mean what they say but you will find that the situation has changed very much. You will find that our Indian brothers now are coming to the forefront of nation building. Look at our Assembly Speaker and all these great traders that are giving so many donations for the education of our children and other worthy causes." He looked at the Ambassador with a benevolent face trying to smooth the tense atmosphere.

"No, Mr. Minister," said Sandra. Chozo heaved himself up in the chair to give all his attention to Sandra. By the look he was going to wear he wanted to tell her that he could not wait any longer. By it he wanted to tell her that she was beautiful, clever and loved by him. He breathed hard from the nostrils exuding a pungent jet of lust. His glass of whisky was visibly trembling in his short fat hand.

"Do you really think, Mr. Minister, that the Indian ever pauses to worry about what is really happening to the African he has lived with — or rather stayed with, living is too generous — for so many years? Nor sir, we are worse than the colonials — at least they were honest enough to say they had come to rule, that they despised the natives — but what have we been? Dishonest material, moral and human suckers."

"Sandra," called out the Ambassador.

"Miss Chaudry," cut in Chozo quickly, "You are being very unfair to our brothers and sisters." He tried to think of something else clever to say but his mind was confused by looking at her.

"How unfair, Mr. Minister? You put the problem very well indeed in Parliament the other day. I was most impressed. Did you not mean what you said?" Chozo wriggled at this accusation. He had spoken with heat in Parliament against neo-colonialism and the new cancer of inward exploitation by a certain minority group. He had pleaded that this cancer that was inwardly eating the nation and making it impotent should be stopped before the full force of independence revolved again by inward corruption into the hands of people who did not care a rap about the country. But then he had made this speech to save himself from Mr. Patel's frightening bills. Ambassador Chaudry thought the conversation had gone too far.

"Well, Mr. Minister, I hope you will excuse me — we must push on to the American Embassy — I'll leave you

106

with these bright young things but don't let them bully you."

Chozo looked at the Ambassador with beady eyes of relief.

"I am sorry that you have to leave so early — have a good time."

"Thank you — goodnight."

"Goodnight."

"Goodnight."

Chaudry was sitting looking at everybody with disdain in his eyes. He had had more than he usually drank and it began to tell.

"Do you know what, Mr. Chozo?" he said. "Everyone here is scared to ask the right question — the question that Daddy would not care to answer — would my Daddy let his daughter marry a nigger?"

"No, Chaudry," shouted Sandra. "That is not the question at all — it is this frightening feeling of seeing two cultures doomed to live together not taking the challenge — this acceptance of double standards with the hypocrisy of pretending that it does not exist. The Indian clinging to his and taking the line of least resistance to protect himself and the African in the midst of the turmoil of making sense with what has hit him for the last one hundred years, sitting back biting his finger nails and watching what Mr. Chozo aptly called an inward cancer slowly eating the new cells away."

There was silence as everyone looked into their glasses and pretended to be drinking.

"But, Lombe, you haven't said a word — are you not concerned with all this?" Lombe had been sitting silent afraid to say anything that his Minister might consider critical. He was disturbed by Sandra's presence. It reminded him too much of Miria and all the other problems of his life. Why do people fling their own problems to others after they have failed to sort them out themselves?

"I really haven't much to say, Chaudry. I am here and you are here," he said, lamely. They all laughed at this.

"Let us have more drinks and some music. This is supposed to be a birthday party not a bloody debating society." Chaudry gave drinks and Sandra went to put on a dance record. Sandra came to Lombe and stretched her hands motioning him for a dance. Lombe looked surprised and bewildered. He cast a glance at his Minister. Chozo gave him a slight nod of approval and a flick of the eye which said in so many words that Lombe was expected to do his duty now. They danced slowly and in silence. Lombe could not understand why the girl was so calm and so self assured. She danced gracefully and held his hand firmly in her's. It was a reassuring gesture.

"You are very quiet today, Jonathan Lombe," she said. Lombe always knew that there was something special whenever the brother or the sister called him by his christian name.

"You do have a problem, don't you?"

Lombe was taken by surprise and at first did not seem to know what to say. Did Sandra know about Miria? Had she got news about his financial problems? Had Chozo made a side remark to her that he had sent him to make a "fixture". He began to feel uneasy.

"I did not mean to pry into your private affairs," she said, encouraging him to admit.

"How did you know, Miss Sandra?"

"So you do have a problem," she said, teasing him with her eyes. "Can I help?" The record stopped before he could answer.

"After I have done my duty to my brother and your Minister we shall talk about it," she said. He drifted back to his place. Sandra went to choose another record. He watched her standing over the player — tall and elegant. Her sari flowed about her in slow rippling streams of elegance and beauty. Looking at her made Lombe realise how dirty and filthy and inadequate all his physical presence and inward life was. Did dirt always attract dirt to itself, he wondered?

"What was it like, man?" Chozo asked, wheezing with a pang of jealousy. He managed to give Lombe a wink however to make quite sure what he meant.

"She is a very good dancer, Sir," he said. "I hope you are enjoying the party, Sir?"

"Ha! ha! ha! yes, very much." He pulled himself forward to the edge of the chair. His large stomach fell forward in a heap between his fat knees. The effort made him fume hot gusts of whisky and ginger. He gave a good deep belch. A fat hand went on Lombe's shoulder and fondly squeezed his shoulder blades.

"Don't forget the fixture."

The music had started and Sandra was walking towards Chozo.

"Mr. Minister, may I have the pleasure?"

Chozo gave a loud laugh and patted his knees.

"You really are cruel, Miss Chaudry. How do you expect an old man like me to do your fancy steps?"

"I am always amused at the way you try to make yourself old, Mr. Chozo," she said. The remark put fire into Chozo and he heaved himself up with the nimbleness that only fat people can muster. They set off with Sandra making polite remarks on how her father always enjoyed talking to him and how good it was that he did not shun the company of the youth of his community. Chozo kept on agreeing to everything she said without hearing the words themselves. He was a good dancer normally but dancing with

Sandra had completely disorganized him. He kept on apologising and squeezing her tight next to him. Each time his hand came near to the fleshy part where the sari did not cover the body, he jerked it back to the top of her bottom.

"I hope you are enjoying Chaudry's party?" She attempted to draw him into some talk and distract him from awkward gestures.

"It is wonderful — it is wonderful." He repeated the phrase over and over again. They danced in silence. Chozo was hot and perspiration ran down his face. His eyes glistened. He thought that she was reacting to his slow caresses. His right hand was kneading her bottom with more pressure. The fact that she did not show signs of disgust gave him courage. Breathing hard he brought his head near her ear.

"Did you get my message from Lombe?" he asked. Sandra looked surprised.

"What message, Mr. Minister? That you would be coming?"

"No, that I would very much like to discuss a few important issues with you." She felt like saying no, but then thought she might put Lombe in trouble if he had forgotten.

"Perhaps later in the evening we might discuss the time and place, Miss Chaudry." He gave her a final knead as the record came to an end. He was pleased with the progress made and walked back to his seat with an assured step.

"If you dance like that in Parliament, Mr. Minister, I am absolutely sure that your constituency will vote you back with an increased vote." This was Chaudry, now drunk and sitting with a beautiful cousin on one knee. Chozo liked the remark very much.

"Wait till I ask you to come to my house to see real national dancing, Mr. Chaudry," he said, walking towards where Chaudry was sitting with the lovely cousin. The music started. Chozo looked round sharply for Sandra but only caught her sari going out to the veranda with Lombe.

16

It was difficult to concentrate on his work this morning. He had spent most of the night awake, tossing in his bed thinking about his conversation with Sandra. He had felt afraid to go out to the verandah alone with Sandra but she had a strong will and had given him the strength to do so. She looked different outside with only the natural light of the African night. Somehow she had looked like a person he had known for a long time. She had become a real woman to him. She showed signs of concern, care and weakness. He had felt the impulse to hold and comfort her and tell her how much he appreciated her concern for him.

"I come here often in the evening," she said.

"Why do you do that?"

"I don't know why. Somehow I find Africa overwhelms during the day. But at night I find myself able to communicate with this fantastic country." They sat silent for some time. The noises of the party feebly mingled with the silence of the night outside. One felt the vast

113

mystery of Africa across the large garden way out to the dark hills beyond them. She wondered what happened in the villages and forests at night in Africa.

"In our villages the nights usher in a different world," he said.

She nodded and said, "I noticed this very much that evening we spent at your village. It was like a transfiguration."

Lombe tried very hard to understand what Sandra was talking about. Why did this country have such an effect on foreigners? He had noticed this often with Europeans. They reacted to Africa in many confusing ways but basically two. One group fell in love with it so much that it completely destroyed them. The other hated it to an extreme that turned to violent love. The African in the village simply lived it. The urban African hung in the middle desperately trying to avoid the chasm below with the centre no longer able to hold.

Sandra looked at Lombe and said, "Do you remember that young girl you danced with at the village?" Lombe thought very hard.

"What do you mean? In most of our dances we never dance with any particular person, we all just dance," he said.

"Very extraordinary — I remember it so well, it was most beautiful but frightening as well. But back to your worries. What is the matter?"

Lombe had prepared his speech for Chaudry, not for Sandra. How could he ask for money from a woman? Besides was he sure that he would be able to pay it back in good time?

"I don't know really. But there are so many things happening at the same time, Miss Sandra," he said.

114

"Sandra," she said.

"Sandra," he repeated.

"That's better. Now let's be serious, Jonathan. I have been worried about you for sometime. Are you in financial trouble?"

Lombe could not react to this one. He kept quiet. She understood.

"It is always difficult — always difficult to say things — don't you find it so?"

"It is always difficult," he said. He did not quite know what he meant by that — but somehow it had some profound meaning.

"Tell me, why are you such a sad person?"

She was not looking at him. Her eyes were gazing away into the dark voids of the sky. Her sari shoulder flap had slipped down to her elbow and she was breathing in short spasms that made Lombe feel a pain in his heart. This was no ordinary woman, he thought. She is an octopus. Why was he sad? He himself did not know why all of a sudden he had become such a sad character. When he was an unknown junior clerk things at times had been difficult but life had been easy and carefree. With Sammy and Brute there was nothing much to worry about. He did not have much money but it saw him through each month. His job was convenient. Why were things so different now?

Even Sammy and Brute were now somewhat changed. When they talked it was on the surface. There wasn't any more that friendship of the simple and satisfied that flowered every evening they met at the Astronaut. Now the understandable dark void and ugliness of Chozo, Patel, 'The Stooge', Al of the American Embassy, mixed with the beauty of Sandra and Chaudry. But above all the ever gnawing darkness of Miria. That cut like a razor. It had shown him

115

all the meanness and ugliness of man. How did Sandra expect him to explain all this to her? Could she whose upbringing had prepared her to deal with these complexes understand what it means to have no centre? To jump from one edge of the river to the other without feeling the weight and drag of the water over your body? She turned slowly and looked at him.

"Why are you so sad?" she asked again.

"I don't know, Sandra. It is just many things."

"I like you, Lombe. I like you very much but you are a very difficult person to know. You live so much in yourself and you refuse to accept others simply. It is not good. It always causes tragedies to refuse love."

He had not asked her to explain what she meant by this. The voice that came from her had been a familiar voice and he recognised it. There was no need to ask her for the meaning — he knew the meaning. But it was painful. They spent almost an hour outside. When they stood to go in, her hand reached for his. It was warm and moist. The party had broken up and Chaudry drove him back to his house.

* * *

There were three letters for him on his table that morning. The first was from Sandra containing a cheque for fifty pounds and a small note in a neat handwriting saying that she hoped this would help and he should not think of paying it back as that would be a terrible insult. It also hoped that they would meet again soon. The other two letters were from people claiming to be his relatives, both asking for money as tokens of thanks for the work they did in helping him with his education when he was a small boy.

The internal telephone rang. He had since stopped feeling excited about telephones and files in trays. He let it ring for some time.

116

"Hello, Mr. Lombe?" He recognised the voice. It was the new personal secretary of the Perm. Sec. The affected tone made him feel sick. He could visualise her a tight dress over a shrunken body called slimming. Tottering on high heeled shoes that made the graceful African body look like a hanging body. The voice came lipstick coated with an affected London drawl that had been quickly picked up in six months of secretarial training. Her only qualification against more deserving candidates for being sent to this course was because she had agreed to sleep with the Minister concerned after the interview.

"Yes, Lombe speaking."

"Em, the Permanent Secretary on the line for you." There was a rather amusing foreboding ring in the voice. He had never paid attention to her and she had secretly hated him for it.

"Mr. Lombe, would you please come immediately to my office." Lombe said the yes into a dead phone. It must be something to do with the Minister's tour. He wished he could find an excuse not to go. He had been excited about it at first but after last night he was no longer sure that he wanted to go. He straightened his tie and picked the file on the Minister's tour and went to Kango's office. She was there wearing an outrageous hair style that made her look like a scarecrow.

"Just a moment, Mr. Lombe," she said swivelling in her chair and buzzing a knob on her desk.

"Mr. Lombe awaiting you, Sir. Very well." She turned round to look at Lombe fidgeting with his file.

"You may go in now — Perm. Sec. will see you." The temptation to put her on his knees and give her a good spanking was very great but he thought the better of it.

"O, come in, Mr. Lombe — the Minister wants to see you immediately."

"Do you know what it is about, Sir?"

"You will hear all about it soon." Kango buzzed the Minister's secretary and told her that they were ready for him. She came to usher them in. She was one of those strong-bodied dried-up English women who were invariably the secretaries of all the key men in government. Correct and stiffly courteous from the hips. How government hoped to keep security whilst on the top hovered these ex-colonial dames and majors had remained a wonder to most people. But of course the PM was a stickler for efficiency and he was not going to Africanise for the sake of Africanisation. The fear of leaving mother's apron strings was too big. Anyway to be served and called 'Sir' by a white man enhanced the ego.

"Mr. Kango and Mr. Lombe, Sir," she announced with an air of compressed amusement. She got good pay but habit dies hard. For her to call somebody who looked so much like her houseboy Anyezi 'Sir', was like playing a part in a pantomime.

He chose not to notice them for a cool three minutes. After doodling with a file he picked up the phone and started speaking to another Minister friend of his. Lombe began to have a chill in his body. Was this something to do with the "fixture" or was it simply a show before Kango? He put the phone down after a bilious laugh and decided to notice them.

"O yes, sit down."

"Do you wish me to stay, Sir?" asked Kango.

"Yes, I want you to stay, Mr. Kango."

Chozo took his time to open the conversation. He did not look straight at them.

"Have you got Mr. Lombe's personal file, Mr. Kango?" he asked.

"Yes, Sir, it is the green one on your left."

118

Chozo reached for the file. His fat ugly hands thumbed through the pages. He shook his head as he looked at them. Lombe was tight with curiosity and fear. There must be something wrong.

"It is my great sadness to have first to inform you, Mr. Lombe, that you can no longer come with me on my tour because of some serious matter to which my notice has been drawn this morning." Lombe swallowed hard. Chozo enjoyed every minute of this torture but did not show any outward sign.

"It has come to government notice, Mr. Lombe, that you have taken bribes from certain Indian businessmen of shady character."

Lombe gave a noise of surprise and his mouth made out the name of Gupta.

"You are right, Mr. Lombe, one of them is Mr. Gupta."

"But I don't understand this, Sir," he protested with heat.

You will most certainly understand in due course. These are serious matters." Chozo cleared his throat and continued, "Further, it has been alleged that you have been using your high office to sell some confidential information to certain Embassies." He enjoyed this one and waited for it to sink down slowly and with all the burning pain into Lombe.

"But most serious is that you have been involved in a plot to overthrow the government with a dangerous man normally called 'The Stooge'." A blankness of thought and a paralysis of body overcame Lombe. He remained quiet, looking straight at Chozo.

"I had great hopes for you, Mr. Lombe. But these are serious matters, ones which have disgraced my Ministry. Under the circumstances I have no choice in the matter. Whilst the police are conducting further investigations you will immediately be suspended from your job at half pay to await preliminary investigations. The loan over your car has been suspended and Mr. Kango will make arrangements for it to be taken to the Ministry of Works and Transport for safe custody. That is all, Mr. Kango."

He switched the lights off in his office for the last time and walked back to his government house as the rumours began to spread through the corridors of the Ministry.

17

It was towards the end of the month and so the Astronaut was full. The juke-box blared away louder than usual. It was hot and smoky and smelling as usual of human sweat. Lombe stood at the corner of the building and gave off a loud jet of piss. It made him feel good. The Astronaut presented a world which was neutral. It had not changed much. Of late he had not been coming to the Astronaut often. A senior officer should not be seen too often at these places. You had to make a show at the top club where after siring your Minister and all the top boys you had a chance to get up on the ladder quickly. Lombe had already been drinking and he was going to drink some more here at the Astronaut. He said the name again to himself with relish. 'ASTRONAUT'.

He walked through the door and noticed Sammy and Brute sitting in the corner as usual with a circle of admiring girls. He walked towards them.

"Look what I see," said Sammy. "God almighty himself."

"Jesus — welcome man to this great institution," said Brute. The girls gave Lombe a good look over and decided that he must be a square but with money.

"Sit down, man, and have a drink." He pushed two girls off the seat and told them to go and fetch a cold bottle of beer and a very clean glass for the gentleman. Lombe sat down and warmed to his two young friends. It was difficult to bridge the gap but he knew that he was in good company again. These boys had a core. They lived on their own level — a level which fed the top and bottom level and so maintained sanity for everyone.

"God, it's good to see you, boy," said Sammy, feeling a bit awkward to claim battery charging from them after weeks of separation.

A dark beauty brought the beer and the clean glass. Sammy took the glass and playfully went through the mime of polishing it. They all laughed. The dark girl laughed too.

"She is new and as raw as they come," said Brute.

"She will be alright, I think," said Sammy.

"I don't figure so — she comes from the North — that spells danger for some big what not," said Brute.

"Who is chasing her?" asked Sammy.

"The Minister of Constitutional Affairs, I am told," said Brute.

"He certainly has a constitution here," Sammy said. They noticed that Lombe was quiet. He had been following their conversation. It opened more wounds than they knew. Sammy and Brute fell quiet. They knew what Lombe was thinking. They had heard the rumours and checked them through the string of young and old secretaries that guarded the fortresses of Ministers and the security of the state. In fact Brute had obtained the information from Kango's

122

secretary and cross checked with Chozo's Secretary who in her spare time secretly played the Moira game with these nice dark boys. She had told Brute to go and get the information from her house that evening but Brute was impatient. He played sulkily and not to lose him she had surrendered the information. Then Sammy had got working on the police girls, which source affirmed that Chozo had given instructions for a criminal case against Lombe. They had expected him to come to the Astronaut that evening.

"I am rather tired of you girls swarming around me this evening — why don't you go and dance? I'll buy a beer for the bottom that shakes most," said Sammy. The girls giggled and pushed each other to the juke-box. They knew Sammy and Brute. They were generous but they could be mean if they were not treated carefully.

"How's life, man?" asked Sammy. This was the ethics of those who lived on this level. You did not go charging like a bull into affairs that hurt your friends because their hurt is your hurt and their joy is your joy.

"Things are not too good," said Lombe.

"Ya, we have heard, man — rather rough."

"Yaa, rather rough," agreed Sammy.

They ordered another round of drinks. They knew what to do but they had to observe a few minutes of care and silence to show that they cared and sympathised with one of their own although he had deserted them for some time. This type did not have much but everyone was after them for solace and assurance. Ministers came to them because they were scared of them. The unemployed were fed by them because they knew what hunger was. Innocent girls and corrupted girls came to them because they understood. They were the most genuine part of Independence, like the National Flag, because like them it lived in its own element.

"What are you going to do?" asked Brute.

"I don't know what to do — the charges are so ridiculous."

"You must get a lawyer."

"Where do I get the money to pay him?"

"I have an idea," said Sammy. "Why not ask Nkondo to do it? You know what he thinks about Chozo and all this nonsense of frustrating the young under guise of fear. If, as you say, all these charges are not true he will take it."

"Great," said Brute. "We must get cracking on that. Just the sort of thing he would love to do." The tension was beginning to ease a little but Lombe was far from happy. They noticed that he was inwardly brooding about something far deeper than the threat of a court case.

"Tell me, Lombe, was all this due to that Indian piece?" This kind of vocabulary had been currency for Lombe at one time but big files had turned him into a phrase manufacturer. Lombe looked at Sammy and Brute and a sense of liberation overtook him. He wanted to laugh or cry or get blind drunk.

"Yes. I failed to make a 'fixture'."

"A 'fixture'!" exclaimed Sammy.

"Did you say a 'fixture'?" asked Brute. After a pause they saw the joke and laughed out loud.

The juke-box was playing a new popular number. The bar filled with it and the noise subsided as people turned towards it to listen to the hit. The girls were now caught in it. Lombe thought to himself that this was still the Astronaut. What a complex place. What a source of complications in life. Early in the morning the Astronaut will throw all her children off her lap. They will have to fend for themselves. They will feel helpless. The big cars and the fancy taxis will drive off at three in the morning

124

— and all this energy that is inactively wasting itself in the Astronaut will burst through the safety valves and blow lives in one gust of counted minutes. The depression came back again. In all, he saw Miria around the bar. He wanted to talk to them. He wanted to reach out with his hand and say, Miria this is the Astronaut, don't you remember. I am Lombe. He said the words aloud and he stretched his hand to touch a girl whom he thought was Miria, a clumsy gesture which knocked over his bottle of beer. The girl was not Miria — but the face was familiar. Why was she looking at him?

"Careful, man, Lombe," said Brute amused. "Do you want to go in for rape also?" They all laughed.

"Stop having this water, man. Have a shot of gin. You need it. You look quite a sight you know," said Sammy.

"Kristine, go and get us a double shot and ginger, baby." Kristine! Lombe thought to himself. Kristine! Myriad mornings of gutters and smells of dirty human bodies smelling of sex came to him. He gulped the gin down and felt irresponsibly better. Kristine did not say a word to Lombe. He noticed that she was a bit round in the middle. Maybe that is why she is not going to show that she knows me and make a fuss.

"Do you know what, boys?" he said. "I am going back home to the village." They looked at each other with understanding.

"I must go back to the village for a long search — for a very long search — for a very long search," he said to himself.

Brute cut him short. "You are right, Lombe, go home for a time until the court case. It's going to be rough here until then."

Lombe was in a deep state of depression.

"I must go back to the village for a long search — search." These were the last words that Lombe said at the Astronaut that night. The rest was delirium which he never heard and it was two words — pushing out of him like the working of piston rods — Miria — Sandra — Miria — Sandra.

18

Lombe's village had received the news of Lombe's son before he got there. Some old friends and elders met the bus when it arrived. Everyone was polite and happy to see him in the manner in which one of their family had come back. It was difficult to understand the ways of the town but they knew rather vaguely that Lombe's son was in some kind of trouble with the government and all they could do was to help. This was the duty of the clan. Pity that the young man had not come home more often to consult the elders of the clan and strengthen his juju.

"It is this Christianity," one old man had mused at a beer drinking party.

"Life is too fast there for our boys and all those Europeans working under them."

"Somewhat unnatural don't you think?" There had been silence then another said.

"I have been an elder of the church myself. For a long time — but how could I have survived without you, my friends and the spirits of our ancestors?"

"It is all rather unnatural — such a fine young man to have done so many things."

"Yes. These days," sighed another after a long drink from his calabash.

"I am sure it is due to this other thing," suggested yet another with a wise look.

"It must have something to do with this other thing." Everyone had referred to Lombe and Miria as this other thing. Whenever it was discussed in public it was always referred to as the other thing.

Lombe did not say much to them. They walked to his mother's hut making conversation which included him but which did not require him to say anything. His mind was set. He must find where Miria was. His mother was sitting in her hut doing some house chores. She looked older but composed. Lombe was very moved about her and felt the love of a son for his mother rising in him. After formal greetings they were left alone.

"You must be hungry," she said. "I must get your cousins to make you some food."

"Yes, mother, I am hungry. I need some food." He wished that she would make the food herself. He had missed her cooking for a long time and now wished he could see her cooking the food and once again imagine himself following her all over the compound while she did it. She went out to order one of her cousins to prepare food for her brother. He noticed how this once little girl had suddenly grown into a woman. The girl had now developed firm breasts and carried her body like a full flower ready for pollination. She wore that shy look of the village girl that was greatly prized by the community. She had looked at him with admiration. He thought of the brush jerky manners of the Astronaut girls. They had been like this once. Then they went to the cities. The blooms had been snatched and the ripe ovaries had been left bloomless — mere round stubs on which the bees alighted and finding the nectar gone flew away. Rotted with disillusion; after that rotted by the germs that passed from one to the other in these cities. Then the rot caught the heart and the heart became hard; like a rock.

The word had quietly gone round that Lombe was at his mother's house. Food began to arrive from the homes nearby. This was the custom. One welcomed strangers and especially relatives because they belonged. This thing that had fallen on Lombe's house had fallen on all of them. It was their duty to see it through and finalise it properly. This awe inspiring concern of man for man is what the big people in the big new government in the big city had been trying to write down. They had given it a big name, 'African socialism.' They had mixed it and patched it up with a lot of other big ideas from unknown countries. They had violently yoked it to all sorts of other ideas and called it 'Policy' and now landrovers and loudspeakers with recorded music came each week to explain it to the people who lived in Lombe's village. They listened patiently to the young pioneers in their uniforms and party slogans. Children playing at toy soldiers explaining to them the wisdom of the old. The old women of the village had been made to dance to these young gods in praise of this new thing called 'Socialism' — others called it 'Progressive Communalism.' Then the smart and strong and very powerful young children called the pioneers had demanded chickens, cards and organisation and had left to report to Chozo their great success after beating up a number of old men and women who had not come to listen to their pantomime. Did they not know that if God on earth sends his little angels to send the word, that everyone must come and listen? Food and more food came to Lombe's hut. A few remained for a few minutes to exchange greetings and snatches of conversation with Lombe. Soon he relaxed and took off his jacket, tie and shoes.

Much of this food was not going to be eaten by Lombe. Everyone knew this. He tasted as much as he could and sent it to the children waiting outside. They had a field day of eating. In this way they learned that strangers and relations coming back are important parts of their way of life. The cousin brought the food that was for him. She put it down in front of him and with a shy lift of her eyes invited him to eat. Lombe tensed up — she looked so much like Miria.

It was late in the evening, when he was sufficiently rested, that his mother came to the hut where he was to stay. She came in quietly, giving him the reverence that is due to a grown up man and a son.

"I hope you have had enough to eat?" she said.

"Yes, mother, more than enough and all very good."

"I am pleased to hear that. All you town boys always look hungry." He gave a nervous laugh at this. In her youth she was respected as the best girl of her age group.

"I am not surprised that under your guidance my cousin cooks so well." She said nothing to this. A shadow of pain passed across her face and she looked down on the ground. Lombe did not understand why this remark of obvious praise did not please her. She kept on looking at the ground and making attempts at continuing the conversation.

"I hope you will stay long with us this time?" she said.

"No, not very long, mother."

130

"That is sad — we thought you had come for what you called your long stay."

"Well, it would have been my long stay, mother — but I have got to go back to some important business." She looked away from him. Her face had suddenly grown tense, tired and old. Lombe felt a strong feeling of shame and compassion.

"Yes," she said. "We have heard about that my son. There is nothing that man can say," she added. "God is there." In these last words, 'God is there,' she had said all that she wanted to say. In them she had established his innocence. In them she had asserted that it was the jealousy of others in these evil towns against her son's progress that had brought this up. But God was there and everything would in the end be righted. Her son might be innocently made to suffer for this but eventually those responsible would suffer more for it. This was fate and justice.

This inner perception was strong in these women. Lombe felt there was no need to explain to her about Gupta 'his prend' or Chozo and the 'fixture' or the many myriad things that if explained would sound silly and out of place in this presence.

"How are your friends, the ones you brought here?" she asked.

"They are very well, mother — they remember you."

"They are very good people." She thought a bit and then added, "And the girl?"

"She is well, mother."

"She is a fine person."

"She has been very helpful to me, mother." She nodded her assent.

"Do you see her often?"

"Many times." She gave him a quick look to read his face.

"Does she cook for you?" Lombe was baffled by this question. What did his mother mean by this odd question?

"So you have met her people," she said.

"Yes, mother — I know her brother well."

"I see," she said. It was a sign that the subject could be put away. She had found out what she wanted to know and had given her verdict. They sat silent for some time, each nursing their thoughts. Each feeling the warm and pained comfort and love of the other. She thought of him as that boy she had held in her arms so lovingly at the most difficult period of her life. His father had almost cut him off by then. He had been the only source of joy. And then he had gone away to the towns and each time he had come it was only for a week or a few days and gone again. Coming back grown and different, talking a different language. She had always kept his image as a baby; that is why she did not want to look him in the face too often.

He remembered her clearly as a very handsome woman. Each time he saw her on his visits he remembered the days of his boyhood and her nice smell of youth and vigour. She still had that streak of sadness in her face. He could not, however, take the pain of her growing old with lines of sadness now showing clearly on the forehead.

"Your uncle will be coming to see you soon," she said. He had expected this but he had to ask her one question before she went. He could not sleep without knowing the answer.

"Mother."

"Yes, my son."

"Please tell truthfully."

"Yes, my son — what is that you want to know?" He

132

looked at her straight in the face for the first time. She did the same too.

"Mother — is Miria here?"

She did not take her eyes off him. Speaking through him to some power away she said, "You'd better ask your uncle about Miria."

She left the hut as Lombe's uncle's footsteps were heard outside.

19

He was an old man who had seen life. In his village
he had prepared himself to live a full life. But the change
came. It was not a sudden change. A white man with a book
in his hand. Every evening this white man with the book
had sat at the edge of the village and played with the
children. Joked with them until he had learned the language.
Then he launched on the old people and started talking to
them about strange Gods and strange countries. They had
listened patiently to him. Then he started to teach the
children the strange marks in this book. He taught them to
sing new songs. Songs which put you in a straightjacket
until the only way in which you could sing them with
enjoyment and meaning was to distort them completely.

Then other white men came and the young men began to
disappear into far places leaving the old people to look after
the land and after their women and the old men died
without comfort. He had known all along, as he kept on
telling his friends, that something terrible would come out

of all this some day. And now this thing had come. He knocked at the door of the hut.

"Come in, Uncle," said Lombe.

"Thank you, my son," he said. "You knew I was coming?" Lombe offered him a stool. The old man fussed around trying to compose himself. One had to be careful with these young boys these days — they had tongues of fire and he did not want to enrage this thing again. If he failed that would be the end of the village.

"It is good to see you again, my son," he said.

"It is good to see you in good health, Uncle."

"Yes I have been lucky, my son; but my days are going fast."

"No, Uncle, you still have the strength of a bull in you." This pleased the old man very much. He fussed around again laughing quietly to the young man.

"You young men have always got fine words to us old ones." He liked the way the conversation had started. The boy definitely wanted to talk and this was good.

"And what is the news from the big city, my son?" he began cautiously. Feeling his way into the subject with the courtesy of the court that had brought him up.

"Not much, Uncle, besides what you have all heard," Lombe said.

"Yes, my son, we have heard many things. But words are sometimes like all stories unless one hears them from the story teller himself."

Lombe wanted to ask him the vital question. He had to hold himself or the old man would clamp down until he felt he was ready to talk like a man. These matters were too important and heavy to be rushed. It was this rushing about like a bush fire that was consuming the young people he would say.

136

"Well," continued the old man. "We have not heard much here, but what we heard has sorrowed our hearts." Lombe made no comment. The old man liked this because he found it irksome these days to argue with the young. He wanted his peace. Whenever those young boys called the pioneers had come into the village and shouted about, asking him to play the drum so that the women could dance, he had obliged without question. He had played and the puppies after more noise had clambered into their cars and left the village in peace.

"What you have heard, Uncle, is true. I am in trouble but it is all wrong."

"You speak like your father. He was not one to talk round the point. Of course, I believe you, my son. I believe you." Lombe thought over the old man's words. Why should he believe so quickly? What does he know about the sharp knife that cuts into the towns and destroys innocence?

"But why should these things come to me, Uncle?" asked Lombe. The old man chewed at his toothless gums and spat in the corner of the hut. He took a generous helping of snuff from a piece of cloth and put it deftly between the lower lip and the gums. He chewed and then gave a good sneeze directing the jet against the wall. He used the back of his hand to wipe off the tears that always came into old men's eyes. The palm wiped off the mucus from the nose.

"You ask why this thing should come to you — why does anything come to any man? Things come because of things that came and so it goes on, my son." He paused to consider his words. Lombe waited, impatience welling in his heart.

"How are the white people you brought here?" he asked with much interest.

"They are all well, Uncle — they remembered you."

"That is good — they are very good people — and the girl?" he asked.

"She is very well, Uncle."

"That is also very good."

Lombe wondered why Sandra had been singled out in these enquiries.

"My son," continued the old man, "no man can crack lice with one finger."

"It is true, Uncle."

"This that has happened in the town has brought you back to help us to crack this lice."

At last the old boy was coming to the point. Lombe could not wait any longer.

"You mean, Uncle, what happened between me and the girl of my home town?" asked Lombe with some heat. He was beginning to get warm all over the body now. The old man bid his time. He did not look at Lombe.

"I thought so — just like your late father, always quick-tempered and impatient. You are right, my son. That which happened between you and the girl of your people is what has brought you all this to bring you here," he said.

"I do not understand, Uncle."

"I know, my son — who ever really understands anything in the heart of a man? We all live to ourselves until something brings us together. But here in our village all belongs to our total life."

It was time for another dose of snuff. Too many words together always tie up the mind and hide wisdom.

"Where is she, Uncle?" Lombe asked. This to help the agony of asking the old man to mention the name of Miria.

"Why do you want to know, my son? Should we not put that aside now, my son?"

138

"I can never put that aside, Uncle. I came here to see her," he said. The old man sat up straight. His eyes shone from the semi-darkness of the hut lighted by a fire. He held up his head with the pride of a lion showing contempt for Lombe.

"You came here to see her, my son?" he asked with what seemed like the roar of the lion. "You came here to see her, my son?" he repeated. Lombe saw the fire in the old man and was frightened.

"Yes, Uncle, I came here to see her," he said.

"The foolishness of the young. You came here to be saved and now you want to destroy all of us," he said with anger.

"I do not understand, Uncle," he said.

"All cowards always say they do not understand when they take the course of destruction."

The old man took another pinch of snuff and gruffly stuck it under the lower lip and gave a loud sneeze that sent real tears rolling down his cheeks. He wiped them off slowly. Deliberately made it clear to Lombe that he should now speak like a man and not like a sentimental town boy.

"We pray to our ancestors to save you from the destruction of the white woman and now you come here to destroy us all," he said to him, anger shaking his body.

"I want to see Miria, Uncle," he said in a final tone. The old man realised that he had no power over this passion.

"Do you know Miria, my son?" he asked in a slow soft voice of fear. Lombe did not reply to the question. Did he in fact know Miria? The only thing he knew about her was that she came from his village and was at the moment carrying his baby. That without seeing her and telling her that he wanted to marry her life would be worthless.

"You don't know, my son; you're thinking with your blood. I will tell you," the old man said. He shifted in his stool to make himself comfortable. This thing was going to hurt. He had been chosen to settle it — to bring it to an end before its powers of destruction were let loose. This boy did not know what he was doing. He fixed his sorrowful eyes on Lombe — pleading with him to listen and take his advice. He was too wise to miss the fire in the boy and the stubbornness of his father.

"Do you know the young girl who brought you food today?" he asked.

"She is my cousin," he said.

"My son, she is not your cousin," he closed his eyes and said. "She is your sister."

"But that is the same, Uncle," he said with impatience.

"Yes, my son, she is of course the same," he said.

"Then why do you ask me?"

The old man looked at him with pity and compassion. How could he make him see the point without letting loose the powers of destruction. These boys who had been uprooted and grown without any real roots — how could he make him understand without letting the powers...

"Tell me, my son," he said. "Whom does she look like?" Lombe calmed down to think. He took some time over it and then it came as clear as dawn, she looked like Miria. But there were many girls in the village who looked like Miria. What was the old man driving at? Even at this moment a certain terror struck Lombe's heart. The old man saw signs of it.

"You remember the night of the dance when you brought the white people? You had no time to notice that it was a special dance. It was the white woman who put a veil over your soul and you could not see. It was the dance of cleansing." Lombe remembered that the dance of cleansing was an important dance but not having been initiated he did not know why it was important.

140

"I know that you do not understand what I mean by the dance of cleansing, how could you, you were busy reading the book from the white man, and then he took you away."

Lombe listened.

"Yes, he took you away and told you that secret stories of superstition are not for the children of his God. Maybe he was right. His God is powerful — look at you now coming to destroy us, my son."

"Destroy you, Uncle?" he asked feebly.

"It was for your father and for you. After marrying your mother, your father got drunk one evening and slept with your aunt. Miria was born. He went mad as a result of this and slept with his sister again and your present cousin was born. We have never seen him since. According to the laws we had to wait for so many years before the dance could be performed. It could not be performed because in the middle of it all Miria, whom the elders had been hiding for some time, suddenly appeared — moved by the ancestors to join the dance. You joined it too because the powers of this evil were in her and you danced together though you did not recognise each other. The only person who did so was the white woman you came with."

"Uncle," muttered Lombe, "are you trying to tell me that Miria is my sister?"

The old man picked up his stick and left the hut.

20

When Lombe got off the bus he went straight to the Astronaut. The days he had spent in the village after talking to his uncle he did not speak to anyone. He had secretly been searching for Miria. She was nowhere to be found. His trial was in a few days time.

The Astronaut looked the same. He hoped to see Sammy and Brute here. 'Julieta', that popular hit, struck him in the face as he blindly walked in. He was thin and dirty from the journey. As he walked in hoping to disappear in the warm friendship of Sammy and Brute the usual noise that accompanied the jukebox stopped as if by order. The jukebox played on — louder than ever asking "Julieta, Julieta where are you?" He reached the counter. Everyone was looking at him. In front of him was a newspaper. He saw the headlines, 'TOP CIVIL SERVANT TO BE TRIED TOMORROW — CORRUPTION AND BREAKING OFFICIAL SECRETS ACT ALLEGED'. Top Civil Servant Jonathan Lombe to be tried tomorrow for corruption,

breaking Official Secrets Act and immorality...' Lombe
gazed at the paper. He looked around the room. He could
not recognise any of the faces. He turned around and left
the Astronaut as the jukebox came to the final question of
where Julieta was.

*   *   *

He did not know how many miles he walked. Several
times he had walked past the Indian Embassy. It stood
there, impressive, mysterious and quiet. The windows were
open. The main gate was closed. He could not see any signs
of life inside. A car came round to the main gate and he hid
behind some bushes. It went in and the guard at the gate
closed the doors again. He passed on and went up the hill
feeling like an animal that was being chased and slowly
cornered. Somehow this large and big world seemed
too small for a small and dirty little man like Lombe. If only
he knew where Sammy and Brute were. He was frightened
of the loneliness of his government house. People would see
him go in and would look at the house curiously. He stopped
at a bottle store and spent the only money he now had left
on a bottle of gin. He fondly put it in his pocket and decided
to go to his house and wait for the police there to take him
to court the next morning.

It was now getting dark with a sharp chill in the air.
Slowly the lights went on in the windows. Lombe watched
them multiply and thought of the many lives within these
lights that were engaged in the problems and joys of living.
He felt very lonely. He remembered the days when as a
youth life did not seem to have such insurmountable
problems, except those of living. If now he dredged his life
he wondered what kind of muck he would draw from it.
He felt no longer repulsed with the idea of having slept with
his sister. Somehow a feeling of intense love and tenderness
came overbearingly over him. He loved her on two planes

144

that made his heart and his whole being ached for her. His whole life was now bent in one direction to find her, to feel her presence again. It was only from that he could achieve balance and sanity of mind. Nothing else mattered except Miria. She held the key to a life that was now smouldering with a consummation of the fire of kinship blood. People talked of the closeness of love between man and woman and between man and man. This was something different. It had the agonies of the pure and the beautiful.

As he walked towards his bungalow he felt a strong power draw him towards something with an urgency that only death draws one towards its last mystery. He staggered on to the house, not noticing people or his surroundings. Some kind of power was directing him towards it and he could not resist. As he went, breathing hard, pictures of Miria and Sandra flashed in front of him — teasing, beckoning and disappearing and he wanted to shout to them to wait. On and on he went blindly towards a house he now recognised. He burst through the door with such force that when he realised he was in a room with a light he jerked himself to a sudden stop of fright and wonder. He looked terrible. Sweat dripped from every part of his body. His eyes stared ahead of him for what seemed a very long time. He stood in the living room for a considerable length of time cooling. Then he heard a groan in the bedroom.

A sudden spasm of terror gripped him. The fear of arriving at the moment of truth took away from him the strength to run away. He stood there watching the door and unable to move any part of his body. His mind raced and reeled in myriad thoughts and visions. Slowly the curtain that covered the inner door parted. A figure came through, walking in painfully measured steps. Lombe looked at it. It was Miria. Lombe looked at her, his heart pounding. She looked at him — weak and heavy with child. She was summoning every fibre of will power to stand. They looked at each other for what seemed like eternity. A timeless moment that only those who know each other intimately can ever experience. Her body began to sag slowly to the ground. She reached out a feeble hand towards the wall to support herself. Lombe sprang up and held her in his arms before she hit the ground. She was hot and trembling in his arms. He was suddenly bathed in a hot sweat that trickled in large drops down his face. Without much effort he lifted her and tenderly laid her on the bed, kneeling and watching her as she lay there with her eyes half closed.

Lombe kept calling her name until she opened her eyes.

"Miria, you are back," he said.

"Yes," she said feebly.

"I've been looking for you."

"I have been looking for you too. It has been a long time."

"You are in pain."

Miria nodded her head. She looked thin and grey. She was breathing in pain. He held her hand. It was very hot.

"Have you had anything to eat, Miria?"

"I am not hungry — thank you, Lombe."

She half closed her eyes as a shaft of pain passed through her body making her muscles tense.

"Miria, I must take you to the hospital."

"There is no point, Lombe," she said. "Let me be here."

"No, I'll go and get a taxi."

"Wait a moment. Just sit with me for some time."

Lombe could not bear the sight of her ill. Her face looked frightening in that great pain. She looked like a person who had seen many things from many strange lands. Nothing on earth could touch her. She began to shake; slowly at

146

first and then more violently. Lombe began to cry and whisper in her ear.

"I love you Miria — I love you."

The words seemed to have a calming effect on Miria. The shaking stopped except for the perspiration.

"I did wrong to leave you, Lombe," she said in a feeble whisper. "Now it is too late. The village wanted to destroy me; they were right but I wanted him so much for you, Lombe. I wanted to have him for you. Do you understand?"

"Miria don't talk like that, you will be well and everything will be alright," he pleaded.

"Perhaps, Lombe, but I have come to release you and everybody."

"You must live for me and for the baby, Miria. You must."

"It is unnatural," she said.

"Don't you love me?"

"You are me, Lombe. How can I not love you?" She turned her face to him and said, "The pain is very big now — can you feel him move?" She took his hand and put it on her navel. Lombe felt the violent move of the baby in her, seemingly wanting to wrench itself out from the inside of its mother. He felt the bulges as it made these violent moves.

"I must go and get a car to take you to hospital." She heard his words from a great distance. Lombe looked at her. Her eyes were closed, her breathing was weak and came in quick gasps. He ran out of the room to stop any car on the road, saying to himself, "She must not die — God please — she must not die." He ran along the road for some time and then saw the lights of a car coming towards him. He tore off his shirt and stood right in the middle of the road frantically waving for it to stop. The car came towards him; he did not give way but waved his shirt like one possessed, shouting at the top of his voice.

The car stopped. Lombe ran to the driver's window and clung to the door shouting, "Quick, she must not die, she must not die. You must take her to hospital."

The driver saw the panic in the man. He shook him hard, shouting back. "I can hear you, what is the matter?"

Slowly Lombe realised that he was talking to Chaudry.

"Chaudry," he called out.

"It is you, Lombe. I was coming to find out whether you had come back. What is the matter?"

"Quick, take me to my house. She must not die."

Lombe got into the car and they drove to the house.

Miria lay still now. Her eyes were closed and her body was very hot. Chaudry saw the look of terror in Lombe's eyes.

"Who is she?" he asked.

Lombe did not reply.

"We must take her to the hospital immediately."

They carried her into the car and drove without speaking to the hospital.

Lombe was not allowed to see her any more. He stood outside in a trance. For a long time he stood there with Chaudry watching him. When it seemed that he would not move away, Chaudry took his hand and led him to his car. He followed meekly like a child.

At the Embassy Chaudry gave Lombe a hot glass of milk laced with brandy. Lombe drank it like a child, holding it with both hands. He sat listening and looking at the door; Chaudry read his thoughts. He said, "She has gone. Daddy sent her away the day the newspapers came out with the story."

21

He had had a restless night. On two occasions he had woken up after vivid dreams of Miria. The first dream was of Miria waking him, she stood by his bed holding a bundle of what looked like a litter of puppies. Miria would not part with them when he had tried to take them away from her. She held them so tight that Lombe thought they would be suffocated. He tried to speak to her but he could not open his mouth. He struggled with her, freeing her hands — but they were firm and tight.

He stayed awake for a long time after this dream. His thoughts wandered around trying to knit his life with Miria. But being in Chaudry's house he felt a close presence of Sandra. Miria and Sandra seemed to merge into one person. Why had she left without leaving a message? He remembered the night on the veranda. That was the closest that he had ever come to knowing her. It was that evening that he had realised fully how much he loved Miria. How all this time all the worthwhile thoughts he had had for Sandra were

151

really thoughts he had for Miria. Sandra had been Miria's shadow, the shadow had now gone and he could see Miria in a sharp perspective. It was painful to think back to the time when she lived with him. He had taken it all for granted. All that had been wasted time. He thought of the night of the quarrel and the way he had beaten her. The thought disgusted him. He prayed for Miria and the baby. He made a vow to himself now only to live for Miria and the baby. If he was convicted and put into prison he would ask her to wait for him. The idea of parting again from her was unbearable. He thought of running away from the country and asking Miria to follow him after the birth of the baby. He felt sure that he could establish his innocence.

The second dream again woke him up violently. He dreamt that he was in Miria's ward watching her deliver the baby. The doctor had turned to him, slowly holding something in his hands. The doctor's face had changed. The mask made him look like a devil and his cap looked like a pair of horns. He handed the bundle to Lombe. Lombe held it. It was a baby with the head of an old man, it had no hands.

After this dream Lombe could not go back to sleep again.

At about three in the morning Chaudry burst into his room in an obvious state of excitement. Lombe sat up in bed.

"What's is the matter, Chaudry — burglars?"

"No, Lombe, not burglars — something more serious."

"What is it?"

"There has been a coup — we've been expecting it for some time."

Lombe did not understand. What was a coup? he wondered.

"What do you mean, Chaudry? What is this thing that has happened?"

"A coup," repeated Chaudry. "The government has

been overthrown by the Army and the Police."

"You mean that the Chiefs of the Army and the Police are now ruling the country?"

Chaudry nodded his head. They sat silent for some time. Lombe was thinking of Miria at the hospital. Chaudry spoke first.

"I am afraid some Ministers have been killed and the whereabouts of other Ministers is at present unknown."

They fell silent again. The early morning light was beginning to lighten the room. Cocks began to crow. In the distance they could hear the occasional gun shots and the heavy revving of army lorries moving into position.

"Old Chozo was killed as he tried to run away from his house," Chaudry said.

"Chozo has been killed?" Lombe repeated the words with horror.

"Yes."

"And the Prime Minister?"

"I can't tell you much but we know he is safe somewhere. General Masauko will be making a statement on the radio in about half an hour's time from now."

"Poor Africa," said Lombe. "Isn't it tragically funny that after all those glorious days of fighting for freedom, now that we have it we behave like a couple of dogs — fighting when there is enough food and to spare for everyone."

"I am afraid it is usually the case, Lombe. Before Independence very few people have the time to examine the new responsibilities ahead; to search their hearts and prepare their souls for the work ahead."

"Power," whispered Lombe between his teeth. "What is wrong with power?"

"There is nothing wrong with power, Lombe. It is man

153

who is always wrong. If you put the wrong man in power then the tragedy embraces all."

"It all seems so bad and humiliating." Lombe sat up straight on the bed and as if speaking to himself he said, "Poor Chozo. An excellent head prefect at school. A keen sportsman. Each time he spoke at school debates and at political meetings before Independence the virtue and principles of the man stabbed you so sharply that you could not go back to your bed and just sit down."

"I understand what you are trying to say, Lombe."

"I admired and believed in that man. He had so much ability to speak and live and suffer for so many other people. Then power came." Lombe paused for some time reflecting on visions of thoughts as they fleeted passed his mind. The great moments of the struggle for Independence. The people packed full at meetings. The great moments of dedication. The many who had died and given courage to those who had wavered.

"Did you ever look at Chozo carefully?"

"Why, Lombe?"

"He could never look at anyone straight in the face. His eyes had that look of people who are half mad — the eyes of a man who has sanctioned death but never felt the sticky slime of blood on his hands. Do you understand what I am trying to say?"

"I know what you are trying to say, Lombe. Power is a complex disease."

"My God it must be, Chaudry. It must be. Somehow one does not feel the tragedy of the death of a man like Chozo because he had ceased to be one. Don't you think that is odd?"

"People who died in greatness are few, Lombe. To die with power and to die great is the honour of a few geniuses."

154

"What a waste. I feel so empty, I have never felt so much guilt."

"What do you mean you have never felt so much guilt?"

"Can't you see it. Don't you see that I am part of this waste? We all saw people like Chozo turning into beasts. They needed our help, but instead we sat down with them drinking and procuring girls for them, afraid to speak out, watching them destroy themselves and all the beautiful things our people stand for. The spirit of this country has been so torn and messed about that even in the village where power at least could be forgotten for some of the time the people are living in a make believe world. No roots of the trusting community."

"I think you are exaggerating a bit, Lombe. There were some good men in that cabinet," Chaudry said with little conviction.

"The good had no chance, Chaudry. No chance at all. We let them down. There they sat either quiet or repeating the words of power." Lombe got up and walked to the window.

"Who was it that said that hero worship of a dictator is a dangerous thing because to a dictator the only thing that matters is success — at any cost?"

"I don't know — I wonder whether people like Gandhi, if they had lived long enough after Independence, would have provided us with an explanation of why after arranging the rose bowl man then put the boot on it?"

"It is time — shall I switch on the radio?" The voice came through. Clear as usual as if nothing of importance had happened.

"This is the national radio. Standby for special announcement. Good morning everyone. This is General Masauko of the national army. I have today removed from power the government. This was made necessary for the good of the nation. Over the past three years much harm has been caused by the people you elected to rule you. Not only has there been corruption, murder and injustice but their policies and love of power had forced them to use all means to destroy the people. A whole generation of young people has been turned into monsters, trained to be destroyers of lives and destroyers of the souls of our formerly simple and great people. Foreign killers from abroad for reasons of their own took on the responsibility of performing those tasks and the nation now will have to live through a generation of citizens whose values no longer exist but simply function blindly for the ambitions of a handful of people to whom the only achievement was power and the retention of power."

The general went to give details of how the army was going to rule until such times as it thought fit that a civilian government could be trusted to rule for the people. "A twenty four hour curfew will be enforced today. Only persons with official duties will be allowed to leave their houses today." The broadcast came to an end. Martial music was played. It sounded strange and unreal. Here in the heart of Africa listening to the void of European martial music. In the emptiness of hopes for a new identity now a national tragedy of power. Suddenly Lombe sat up and said, "I must go and see Miria."

"You know that it will be difficult with this curfew on, Lombe."

"I must see Miria," he repeated with a firmness that said he was not prepared to listen to entreaties of reason.

Chaudry watched him. He was tense and taunt like a tiger ready to leap at his prey.

"I have tried to reach the hospital by phone but the lines don't seem to be working. I am sure she will be alright."

"She must be alright — she has to be alright, Chaudry." Chaudry went over to where Lombe was standing. He put a hand on his shoulder and gently motioned him to sit down.

156

"Tell me to go to hell if I am being nosy. Miria means much to you. You never told me about her."

"No, Chaudry," Lombe said. "I never did and now I wish I had done so. It was all so difficult and confusing."

"I understand; go on."

"There is nothing to tell really. The only person who can explain it to you and me is not here."

"You mean Sandra?"

Lombe did not answer. Chaudry shifted from his seat uncomfortably. He saw the image of his father. Distinguished, learned and secure in the values that had brought him up. He had always tried to emulate these qualities but came out with the shock of suffocation. Lombe had been like an open window to him. His simplicity had appealed to him but more so the seriousness that went with the simplicity. He was shocked the previous evening to find Lombe with a girl in his room. For some time now he had associated Lombe with Sandra. Not in an intimate way but in a beautifully platonic way. He had never imagined for instance that they would ever go to bed together. Their relationship was the meeting of universal beauties in human beings. The relationship that had no rules and can never be explained but is feared by people because it has the means of destruction. So people simply watch it in terror, afraid to touch it. Admiring it secretly but frightened of its immense powers.

"She was very fond of you, Lombe," he said.

"She was a great friend," he said.

Lombe did not want to discuss Sandra. He simply wanted to feel the presence and not try to analyse it.

"My father had to make her go. Her connection with you and the pending court case might have provoked her to do something strong."

"Why don't you use the proper word — embarrassing?"

"I did not mean that, Lombe. It is just that you never

157

know what women will decide to do. I am ashamed that I stood up and watched it happen. I have not been able to think clearly myself since then. I betrayed you."

"No, Chaudry, you did not betray me."

"What do you mean I did not betray you?"

Lombe looked at his friend as if he was seeing him for the first time.

"That is the major problem of our time and generation. Our personal lives are too closely linked with so many challenges that most times we even lose sight of ourselves. Our elders at least had causes. They had the great wars to fight. They came back with medals and wounds. They could live the rest of their lives looking and talking about these things. You and I have only ourselves and lots of great ideas which we can't do much with because our elders have now made them their new causes."

"Were you married secretly to Miria?" Chaudry asked.

"Yes and no. I mean how can one give an answer to such a question? Life would be too easy if our generation could give answers to such questions. You know the story of Mary watching Jesus at the foot of the cross."

"Yes, what about it?"

Lombe could not understand why this vivid image had suddenly come to his mind. He could see and feel it. He could understand the power of the involvement of the man on the cross. The involvement of the woman below. It was one clear picture of so much painful harmony. Some called it basically christian. But it really was not. Then he remembered the picture of Buddha sitting in what he thought were beautiful but impossible positions. The lack of this involvement and yet the immense power. Could one give an answer or an explanation to the crucifixion?

"It is not what it is about it, I think," he tried to explain. "It is the thing itself — just the thing itself."

158

"I am afraid I do not quite understand, Lombe — you may have something which I cannot see." He thought about the rather lame explanation. "It is not what it is about. It is the thing itself." Chaudry thought that this reminded him of the words of advice he had received from his European friends before coming to Africa. "It is impossible to understand them." "They refuse to think out a serious problem and usually simply reduce it to some childish explanation." "Even the brilliant eventually are simply juveniles." This did not come out often when he talked to Africans. The feigned stupidity of the embassy chauffeur for instance — laughing off problems and pretending to be a child when one tried so hard to treat him like a man. He could not understand this refusal by the African to accept a man of another race seriously. It was infuriating because it tended to expose one's pretensions — one's set pattern attitudes and reactions. Maybe that is why many regard the educated African as being treacherous. He knows our forms, at least the European forms and can play at them so well and yet always he is miles apart — years away.

"Do you remember the night of the dance at the village?"

"Yes," said Lombe trying to discourage Chaudry. "Why?"

"Miria was there, wasn't she?" There was a plea in the question.

"Yes, she was there," he said in a matter of fact way.

"You did not introduce us."

"No, I could not."

"Why did you not introduce us to her, Lombe?"

"You are right, I did not introduce Miria to you. I did not, I do not know why. Now that you mention it I wonder why I did not do so. I should have done it, shouldn't I?" Lombe felt helplessly lost. "I should have done the introductions. I should have done them. That would have made you feel comfortable with my mother and all the tribal set up and everybody around us. You wanted that, didn't you?"

"Secretly, Lombe, I wanted you to do it. It was not easy to talk to your mother or the people around us. One could pretend and one wanted the show to be a success. You would do the same thing, Lombe, wouldn't you? I was frightened and I wanted you and me to be a success. Both of us wanted to be a success. We nearly all became a failure until Miria came to dance."

"Miria did not come to dance, Chaudry. You are trying to say that Miria came to dance. She might have been trying to do that, I do not know. You seem to know — tell me why." Chaudry tried to make a sensible remark over this one. He felt trapped over what Lombe was trying to say.

"You want me to be an enemy over this one. It is easy and I would enjoy being one. I would like to be one because everyone else would feel freed from the load that we are all frightened to carry."

"You are a missionary. I cannot understand missionaries and they frighten me."

"They frighten me too. But everything in my life has been associated with values that are missionary. Some call them cosy — comfortable and easy. You have asked about Miria and the dance in the village. It fascinates you. It provides maybe an easy answer — but you are scared to talk about the most important thing. A thing which involves not you and me but two people that you and I have refused to know and understand."

"What do you mean?"

"No meaning, Chaudry. You can explain meanings because you have been brought up to explain things. I do not, I live them. It is harder. It does not make meaning to you, if it did it would cut all communication between us and the tragedy would be that it would cut off the wisdom of

160

your father. But he is a good man and a wise man and who wants to cut off wisdom that demands respect?"

"But, Lombe, she was there. She was there dancing. Not in the way that we all understand dancing — no — but telling everybody a story. You were frightened of accepting the story — I do not know why?"

"The story could have been for you, it could have been for me, it could have been for herself. You ask me the impossible. I should laugh and brush it off. All very easy. Are you not like most of the other people in this country all trying to ask me the key question and then through mystery expecting me to give you the expected answers pat on a gold plate?"

It was day. The light fought through the rich curtains to cut off the mystery of darkness. The guns came through the distance of the embassy and the people with the diplomatic decorum that cuts off man from being. The magic was broken.

"You mean to say that she understood and we did not?"

"She might have done. I do not know. That is a coward's answer — does it not please you?"

"And Miria?" Chaudry asked.

"I think so. You see people like Miria accept their role in our present complex," said Lombe.

"And what is this role?"

"To lie on the altar and be sacrificed. We say many things, we explain and try to justify them, we plan expansively and preach new gospels for people like them. Exhort them to new endeavours, for what?"

"Surely for progress."

"Yes, I know all that," Lombe said rather curtly. "And when all the roads and hospitals are built; when all the schools are full and the pipes bring the water to the village communal tap; when the national airways hum and the sirens blow to clear the way for the new Messiah one still asks what is the meaning."

"And what is the meaning?"

"A good question, Chaudry. It is with those that we are putting on the altar. Frankly our interest in all this feverish inadequacy which we have named progress is merely personal desire to shine before the altar. We burn the soul, watch it reduce to ashes while we admire ourselves in the glow of the priest's robes."

"I wish I could understand what you are trying to say," said Chaudry.

Lombe looked at his friend and said, "Sandra did."

22

The element of curious joy in Africa is electric and terrifying. It is secret and only comes through oblique innuendoes of conversation. Maybe sometimes after the turn of a phrase, the mere flick of a gesture. Most times it is covered by the joy of playing the buffoon. This can be irritating to those who are in a hurry to know. Those who want to send the news tingling on the Reuter wires to inform the world at breakfast that Africa has done it again. And so it was this morning as Lombe carefully picked his way towards the hospital.

He picked a route which would not bring him face to face with the army. He could feel the situation and the tenseness of the air. He had met two men who in their quiet greeting had said, "Brother are you not glad that the swines have had it?" The secret understanding between the common. A cruel understanding because it is based on a negative jubilation. Lombe walked on, picking his route as carefully as a General would plan a manoeuvre. Two more miles to go.

The town was clear, but one felt the presence of eyes everywhere. Looking, asking, wondering, curious. He felt them more personally than the sudden appearance of a soldier holding a gun.

The vision of Miria alone at the hospital pushed him on. He was desperate and he had to see her. How was she? Had she got the news of the coup? He saw three civilians in front of him. They were standing talking at a corner of a building. From the way they dressed he guessed they were the usual town folk. Maybe unemployed or engaged in some kind of peddling trade. He walked on towards them. They looked at him as he approached — putting on an air of ignorance. He was about to pass them when a voice said, "Hey, brother — where are you going to?" Lombe stopped. He looked at them and then said.

"What is it to you where I go?"

The three looked at each other and laughed. Then one said, "I was only asking, but since you are such a brave man to walk on this day we apologise." Lombe did not know what to say to this.

"Don't speak to the man like that — maybe he doesn't know," said one of them.

"Maybe indeed he doesn't know," said another.

"He walks like one who knows — he may be a government man."

"He may be a government man," the other said.

They looked at each other. Lombe looked at them. He was worried about the air of suspicion that hung around them. He wanted to assure these people that he was one of them. That he was going to the hospital to see a very sick person.

"I am going to the hospital," he said.

They looked at him with pity in their eyes. Suddenly

they understood and wanted to help. A warmth of understanding caught the group. How odd, thought Lombe, that Africa always brings back our souls in situations of human concern.

"Is someone ill?"

"Yes, very ill and I must see them," he said.

"My brother, it is dangerous — the soldiers are all over the town and they are very rough today."

"They say they have taken over the government."

"They have also killed a few politicians. They say people must not walk today."

"I have heard the news," he said.

"And you are walking to the hospital?"

"I must go and see my sick relation. He is very ill."

This was a lie. He did not want to tell these people that he was going to see a sick woman. They would not believe him. Maybe they would laugh at him. The three left Lombe to confer in mumbles together. Lombe watched them talk and occasionally look at him. They finished their discussion and came to Lombe.

"It is dangerous to go this way. You must go and see this sick person. We belong to the radical wing and are here to help the soldiers to catch people who are trying to run away. We shall take you to a place where you can wait until you can go to the hospital to see the sick person."

Lombe did not know whether to trust them or not. He had no choice — he followed them. One of the men motioned to Lombe to follow him. They walked without talking, picking their way carefully behind houses towards the African part of the town. Occasionally they saw clusters of soldiers guarding government buildings. They looked tough and impersonal. They seemed to enjoy what they were doing. Yesterday this part of the town was full of people.

Dirty children sprawled in all these backhouses and lots ran along the foot paths.

"Come this way," the man said.

"I shall leave you in this house under the care of some gentleman who will help you to get to the hospital."

"I thank you very much, my friend."

The location was familiar to Lombe. It was very near the house of the girl Kristine.

"Don't be afraid," he said. "I know who you are and the people I am taking you to are known to you."

Lombe took a close look at the man. He had seen him before — he had seen him often. Recognition came, he had seen him often at the Astronaut. He usually sat in one corner drinking his beer slowly and deliberately. He hardly ever talked to anyone. Occasionally he would go out with one of the girls. He had never paid any particular attention to him.

They stopped in front of one of the houses and he knocked on the door. The door was flung open at the special knock. The man went in and Lombe followed. It was semi-dark. All the curtains were drawn. There was a strong smell of beer and people. Lombe made out five or six people sitting down playing cards and drinking beer. The man went to an inner room while Lombe waited. After some time he came back and told Lombe to follow him.

"You will be safe with him — he will help you."

Lombe looked at his new help. He could not believe himself. It was Sammy.

"I will go now," the man said.

"That is fine, Gombe — thank you for the job," said Sammy. When he left, Sammy and Lombe looked at each other. Lombe felt like a small boy caught stealing. Sammy was obviously pleased to see his friend again.

"It is Miria," Lombe stammered.

166

"Yes, I know — sit down and have a drink first."

Lombe sat down and watched his friend going out to fetch him a drink. The room was full of loose paper and files. It certainly looked like an office and not a place where one lived. Sammy came back with two bottles of beer and sat down on a chair next to Lombe.

"You look surprised," Sammy said.

"What is all this?"

Sammy looked at Lombe and a shadow of a smile crossed his face. "What do you think it is, Lombe?"

"I don't know," he said.

"Lombe, you are now at the General Headquarters of the Revolutionary Government." Sammy looked at his friend and laughed as he looked at the confusion on his face.

"You are lucky to find me on duty. Do you know the man who brought you here?"

"No, but I have seen him on many occasions at the Astronaut. Who is he?"

"Gombe. Ever heard the name?"

"Yes, some people call him that." They fell silent. Lombe remembered the name Gombe. He was the father of the nationalist movement and was majorly responsible for the attainment of Independence. When Independence came he was in the first cabinet. He had resigned in protest for some inner party matter which the public had never quite understood. Soon after that he had disappeared from the political front. There had been many stories of what had happened to him. The government had swung like a hammer to destroy him at every possible meeting. There had been stories that he had been killed. Others said that he had fled the country. But the mystery of Gombe hung around and people talked in whispers about him. Each time there was a political scandal or demonstration of

167

political excesses the name Gombe had been invoked. Lombe
began to see the connection.

"I know what you are thinking of. What am I doing
here?"

"You are with them," Lombe said.

"Where else could any self respecting person be,
Lombe? For a long time Brute and I thought we ought to
let you in. We were waiting for the right moment.
But events moved too fast."

"Events moved too fast," Lombe repeated to himself.
He had heard that statement for most of his life. First
at school where his European teachers had been so
concerned about the slow progress of the African. Sometimes
he had wondered whether all this was not connected with
an indication of a kind of inadequacy in themselves. He had
heard this voice again after Independence. This time from
the African political leaders. This time the vocabulary
was different. The words came with a hollowness that
frightened. Unlike the exhortations of the teacher they also
asked one to agree and applaud. You gave your soul not
only to live but also to be able to do the little that was
meaningful to yourself and to those immediately around you.
The whole thing seemed to be lived on two levels — the
lie and the contrived.

At one time he had tried going back to the church.
Here he found the shadow so sharp that he had not even
had the courage to run away. He himself kept off and did
not try and reason it out or even rebel. He felt the
weight of the sterility and the impotence of the pomposity
that was around everything. It was like a rubbish dump.
A raging fire had to be put on the whole thing to purify
the steel that would survive.

"It is like the phoenix isn't it, Sammy?"

Sammy looked at him, not understanding. The racy

168

casualness had left him. He looked serious and self assured. A man with convictions but now somehow seemingly frightened of putting convictions into action.

"It is a European story about a bird or some animal called the phoenix. When it is killed or burnt it rises again to a new life from its ashes."

"What a fascinating story," said Sammy. The story caught Sammy's imagination. He turned it round in his mind. He saw images of meaning in it.

"You mean it is like the village blacksmith collecting all the bits of scrap putting them on fire and then forging something new and strong from the weak and rusty?"

"Something like that," Lombe said.

"It is surprising," said Sammy. "We have never talked like this before."

"Events moved too fast," Lombe said with a feeling of bitterness.

"And now we have to begin all over again," said Sammy.

"It is so humiliating to be told that you have got to catch up. To be pushed around by all sorts of human beings. To be told answers and to be asked to accept the solutions. To be continually receiving from all sorts of people kind advice, their money, their conflicts, their bloody shit almost for events to move fast so that one can catch up. Catch up with what? Sammy, tell me why all this prostitution of us? Why do we accept?"

"We are believers of fetishes. Like the old chief in the European cartoons being fascinated by a cigarette lighter. Ten years later the chief tells the white magician to get him one that works at the first strike or lose his life. That is what we want." They both understood the meaning of the riddle and laughed.

"Why did we not talk about these things before Sammy? What was the matter with us?"

"We were frightened, Lombe. Sometimes just not sure of ourselves or even our convictions. But we did do things in a quiet unarticulate way. At the Astronaut for instance we did say much to each other in our own way. The pace kept us together. We had meaning there. Although sometimes I thought that it was like taking a drug. People came to throw life into a junk heap as it were, because there was nowhere else to give it — gold and shit together."

"And now the Rose and the Fire."

"Yes, Lombe, like your phoenix. It had to come. This time the fire must burn the cinders to ashes, the totem poles, the new phony Gods, the lot must go into the bonfire. Then the frightening beauty of the new phoenix as it rises. Can you see it, Lombe, as it spreads its wings, beautiful and glorious over Africa, buoyed by the values that were flung away to 'catch up'?"

"What a beautiful dream Sammy — what a flight of fancy. I want to hold it though, and Miria and the baby in it." The mention of Miria brought them back to the headquarters of the revolutionary committee. Sammy looked at his friend and so the agony of hope and despair.

"Yes, Lombe, and Miria too — and the new generation. When this festered wound is healed by fire we shall all go back to the Astronaut to celebrate a new meaning — and even Sandra will be there."

"And Chaudry."

"And Moira."

"And Ambassador Chaudry."

"And Chozo."

"And Kristine."

"And Gupta."

"And mother."

170

"And father."

"And Konza."

"And Gombe, playing the jukebox."

"And we shall all dance to the jukebox and the tom toms of the village and the sound will have a new beauty."

"And Israel will not train murderers in Africa for Israel."

"And America will bridge the gap of the Atlantic through the catharsis of dredging the festered sore that she dragged across the Atlantic to the new world."

"Stop it, man. It is so silly." They both laughed. They had never been so close. In the distance could be heard the revving of army lorries as they patrolled the new quiet city.

23

Miria died on the night of the coup. The labour had
been long and painful. Through it all she had not made
a noise but her face had shown the pain and agony that
she had gone through. The doctor and nurses had watched
it and worked hard to help Miria deliver her baby. At
first the baby had tossed and turned violently, seeming to
want to wrench itself from the mother's womb with so
much violence that it would burst out like an explosion
of a bomb. Then movement began to slow down. And then
there was no movement at all. Numbness struck the doctor
and the nurses. Miria closed her eyes. Sweat trickled across
the channels of the closed eyes and the lines of pain on
to the white sheets. The doctor motioned to the midwife
for the instruments.

They cut the baby out limb by limb. And when the
baby was out, and all the things that must come out,
the doctor motioned to the nurse to take away the basin
that contained the baby. Miria stretched out a weak hand

which held the doctor's hand with the strength of the drowning holding on a straw.

The doctor tried to look at Miria. He found it difficult to explain. Miria held his hand firmly as the numbed nurses stood frozen holding the basin that held the blood and parts of the baby.

"I want to see the head," she said feebly but firmly.

The doctor and the nurses heard the words but made no movement.

"I want to see the child," she said again. The doctor looked at her — pleading to her not to ask from him more involvement.

The doctor reached for the head from the basin. With cotton wool he dabbed blood from the severed neck. He asked for a towel and wrapped the neck in it so that it just showed the face. It was a puffed up peaceful face of a new born child with its eyes firmly closed.

"I want to see the baby — please," she pleaded.

Slowly he handed it to her.

She took it from him. She looked at it for what seemed a long time. Then as the light began to fail from her eyes she unwrapped the towel from the head and kissed it. As she was near to go she put the head next to her cheek and said, "Lombe."

24

The sister in charge stood squarely and starched in front of the Maternity Ward. Lombe approached her impressed by the white and the spotless cleanliness of the surroundings. The Sister watched Lombe — preparing in her mind the way she was going to send off this man who had the courage to come to the maternity ward out of visiting hours and a time when they were most busy. Lombe sensed the efficient but polite antagonism.

"Can I help you, sir?" the white uniform said with an air of amusement at the normal discomfiture of expectant fathers.

"Yes, Sister. I have come to see the baby," he said.

"You have come to see the baby?" she said. "Which baby?" Trying hard to hide her amusement.

"My baby," he said shyly. She looked at him showing signs of alarm. Lombe thought he should make himself more clear.

"I mean our baby, Sister," he said.

She had handled several cases of this kind before. This must be a new father. They always found it difficult to make themselves clear.

"I see," she said. "And what is your name, sir?"

"Lombe," he said. "Jonathan Lombe."

175

"Will you sit down here and I will go and see if Mrs. Lombe can see you."

She disappeared quickly into the ward; the starch scraping hard against her stockinged shapely legs.

Lombe sat down to wait. Full of excitement he said to himself that this was the day that he was going to tell Miria that his life and hers were now one. He was going to explain to her everything. He was going to be like a child and tell her everything. He would then take her and the baby to the village and to his mother and have everything put right. Then they would all come back to the town and plunge wholesale into the business of working hard for the new government.

The Sister came — impersonal, efficient but understanding.

"I am sorry sir, but we do not seem to have on our list of patients a Mrs. Lombe."

"Miria not here," he said. "But she must be here." The Sister saw the agitation in Lombe's face.

"I'll show you where they put her," he said.

"I am sorry sir, but we do not have a Mrs. Lombe on our list of patients."

Lombe felt weak all over. He stood there looking at the Sister his heart full of anger and fear. Where had they taken Miria. She looked so sure and so confident. This made him feel silly. Then the truth came. Miria could not have been registered as Mrs. Lombe. "You are right Sister — Miria was not put down on your charts as Mrs. Lombe."

"You mean she is not your wife?"

This was too much for Lombe. He could not go into the agony of explanations at this moment. It was the doctor who saved the moment. He recognised Lombe.

"Sister," he said. "I know this gentleman. Will you come this way please." Lombe followed the doctor.

*   *   *

The road to the Astronaut was a long one. Like all the roads of loneliness. At first he had thought of going to Chaudry's. Chaudry would understand and would surely give him comfort. But he did not want comfort, he wanted to feel every bit of the pain. He wanted the pain to be multiplied so that every part of him would feel it. He had to be near people. Any kind of people so long as he did not know them well. He had to keep his mind sane and only the presence of people could do that for him. He walked on and on, drawn by the Astronaut.

The town had filled again with people and traffic. There was an air of festivity. The soldiers on patrol joked with the people. The coup had been well received. The tension had eased. Lombe thought how very much a part of it he had been a few hours ago. Now it seemed strange and remote. A taxi came careering his way. The driver was honking his horn with great relish. Lombe stopped him.

"Yes, Sir, half fare today for everybody."

"To the Astronaut, please," Lombe said.

"Very good, Sir, fine place to go to today," Lombe did not respond to the enthusiasm of the driver.

"Get off the road man — you got to learn to drive good, now freedom come back — bugger!" The driver shouted at a fellow taximan. The other driver smiled back broadly and made an obscene sign.

"Everybody happy today, Sir," the driver shouted back.

"I am glad," said Lombe.

"Yes, Sir." He went on talking to Lombe all the way to the Astronaut but Lombe did not hear any part of the conversation.

As expected the Astronaut was full. Lombe pushed his way in and chose a seat in the corner. It was very much the same but it had also changed. It looked clean. The people who were drinking had not come there merely to get drunk. They talked seriously, they discussed the coup and what was going to follow. They looked genuinely happy. The fat girl came towards Lombe. Her dress was still tight and her bottom wiggled as seductively as before.

"What will you have, Sir?" she said — giving him that look which said I recognise you. You were uppish now you have come back.

"A large beer, please."

He had been drinking for a long time, slowly and steadily. He watched the bar getting fuller and fuller and the noise getting louder. He was away with his thoughts. The presence of the people helped to distract him whenever his mind wandered to thoughts whose fringe he knew he could not bear to think about. He felt a hand on his shoulder. Turning round he saw the gleaming face of Sammy appealing for enthusiastic recognition.

"I thought I might find you here — we have made it boy — we have made it," he shouted.

Lombe looked at his friend unable to say anything and yet now wanting his company.

"What is the matter, Lombe?" he said.

Lombe tried to say something to Sammy, just a few words to cover up the matter until later. Sammy sat down next to him. "Lombe," he said very gently. "Is it Miria?" Lombe nodded.

"It is not very serious, is it?" Lombe could not avoid this question. All the time he had avoided using the word death, he kept on telling himself Miria had not died. People like Miria don't die. Each time the image of death

came to his mind he refused to accept it. He had visited
the graveyard where Miria and the baby had been buried
by prisoners, because she had no relatives to claim the
body. He had looked at the fresh mound of earth
that covered the bodies of a woman and a baby. Both in
standard prison coffins and wrapped by standard government
blankets. He had stood there and come away convinced
that though their bodies might be under that bit of
dirt, Miria and the baby were not there. He saw visions of
them in a world that was part of his and yet unreachable.
To tell anyone that Miria was dead would be to tell a lie.

"It is not very serious, Lombe, is it?" Sammy asked
again with urgency in his voice.

"It really does not matter, Sammy," he said.

"What is the matter with you? Everything matters and
to you above all. Did you see her at the hospital?"

Lombe looked at his friend. He felt a large hot lump
coming up his throat. "No, Sammy," he said, "I did not
find her at the hospital. I found her gone."

"You mean she is..." Sammy did not use the word.
Lombe did not answer the question.

"It is no use my trying to say how sorry I am, Lombe.
It must be tough for you."

"It is very tough, Sammy," he said.

Sammy ordered another round of drinks. "What
are you going to do now?"

"I do not know, Sammy. At the moment I simply wish
to burn. Do not try to put off the fire. I want to burn."
Sammy looked at his friend, seeing a new person.

"Lombe, I respect you," said Sammy. "Do you remember
one day we were talking and you said something about
the involvement of the man on the cross? Now I know
what you meant."

"What do you mean, Sammy?"

"You never knew that I was a rabid nationalist did you?"

"On the contrary, Sammy, I did."

"I worked underground to bring this mess that we have just removed out of power."

"You must be happy now," he said.

"I don't know, it could have been different. The thing is no longer for Sammy's success — thanks to many friends it is for someone I don't know but someone I would like to see."

"What do you mean?"

"Well, somebody like Miria." Sammy felt apologetic and hurt using the name. The fat girl came round and asked them whether they wanted more drinks. Neither replied.

"I am glad you are accepting the fire, Lombe. You remember that story about a bird?" said Sammy.

"The phoenix?"

"Yes, the phoenix," said Sammy. "Miria is that bird."

"Miria is the phoenix." Lombe repeated the words to himself.

"Yes, Lombe — she is that bird, for you, for me and for everybody."

Walking out of the Astronaut one heard drums at night.

PB-37254-SB
5-21T
G

Published by the East African Publishing House, Koinange Street, P.O. Box 30571, Nairobi and printed in letterpress by the East African Institute Press Ltd., Saldanha Lane, P.O. Box 30502, Nairobi, Kenya.